MYS

Tom and Katie cannot understand what's happening in their village. Until recently it had been a thriving fishing port but now that's all changed. The fish have gone; the men are all laid off; the whole place seems to be falling asleep. What's more, all the grown-ups have started to act very strangely. What is going on?

Tom and Katie must get to the bottom of the mystery, especially after finding a strange message washed ashore in a bottle. Someone out there is trying to warn them about terrible things to come. And when everyone starts blaming their misfortune on the seals, Tom and Katie know they have to act. There is something sinister going on, something which could destroy their way of life for ever. Can they stop it before it's too late?

Rosalind Kerven studied social anthropology at the University of Hull. Her books reflect her fascination with different cultures, her sense of history and her concern for the preservation of wildlife. Her affinity with wild northern places has taken her to Lapland, Iceland and the Faeroes, as well as the Shetland Islands. Rosalind Kerven lives in Northumberland.

To James,
     Happy Christmas,
          love
               Tracy,
                  x

Rosalind Kerven

MYSTERIES OF THE SEALS

PUFFIN BOOKS

PUFFIN BOOKS

Published by the Penguin Group
27 Wrights Lane, London w8 5tz, England
Viking Penguin Inc., 40 West 23rd Street, New York, New York 10010, USA
Penguin Books Australia Ltd, Ringwood, Victoria, Australia
Penguin Books Canada Ltd, 2801 John Street, Markham, Ontario, Canada l3r 1b4
Penguin Books (NZ) Ltd, 182–190 Wairau Road, Auckland 10, New Zealand

Penguin Books Ltd, Registered Offices: Harmondsworth, Middlesex, England

First published by Abelard–Schuman 1981
Published in Puffin Books 1989
10 9 8 7 6 5 4 3 2 1

Made and printed in Great Britain by
Richard Clay Ltd, Bungay, Suffolk

Contents

To Nigel
in friendship

I. **A Message from the Sea**

"I'm going to try for another five minutes," declared Katie, "and if I haven't caught anything by then, that's it—I'm going home."

"You might as well go now then," said Tom. "I don't believe there are any fish in this harbour."

"There *must* be," said Katie. "We caught masses here last year."

Tom balanced his rod against a bollard and lay stomach-down on the ancient wooden slats of the pier, peering down into the green, murky water that rippled quietly twelve feet below.

"It's a curse," he said. "That's what people used to say when the fishing was bad."

The sky, which had been thickening with grey, rain-laden clouds all day, rumbled with distant thunder.

"If it's a curse," said Katie, pulling up the hood of her anorak against the coming rain, "we'd better make up a charm or a spell to get rid of it."

"There was once a sort of charm, I think," said Tom.

"Well?"

"You had to chuck someone in the water; and

then the others hauled him out like a fish, to make the real fish think they ought to let themselves be caught too. Stupid, really..."

"Never mind that," cried Katie, "let's try it! You jump in and I'll..."

"No—you!" cried Tom and he pushed her playfully, but harder than he had meant to; she leaped up to give him a hard thump in return. But there was a piece of damp, slimy seaweed lying between them and, as she leaned towards him, her foot slipped on it, she lost her balance and, with a shriek of surprise, went slithering along to a yawning gap where two of the timbers had rotted away in the floor of the jetty.

"Catch me...oh you pig!"

But she could not save herself in time; down she tumbled into unknown darkness, heart pounding, hands grabbing wildly...

...Oh, thank goodness! Within seconds her fingers were gripping something solid—iron beams; then her feet, swinging helplessly in thin air for a few moments, found something firm on which to rest. She took a deep breath and opened her eyes.

"Katie!" Tom's voice floated down from above.

She pulled herself together, looking around her at the shadowy understructure of the pier. It was built rather like a climbing-frame, but all the supports and cross-bars were crusted with a prickly layer of small, dirty-white barnacles, and brown ribbons of seaweed hung limp and lost in the drizzle waiting for the high tide to wash them back to life.

"Katie! Are you all right?"

"Of course I am," she said crossly, as Tom's bedraggled head appeared over the edge of the hole.

"Come back then and help me pack up the rods before they get soaked."

"No, I like it down here! I can see right in."

"In where?"

"In the sea of course! I'm going to see if there are any fish . . . hey, there *is* something."

She eased her way along to the end of the rafter and carefully crouched down until she was just a few inches above the water.

"Hold on, I'll try and reach it."

It was not a fish at all, but something green and round that glinted as it bobbed in and out of the waves.

Katie was good at balancing; but even so she could scarcely grab hold of it without losing her grip on the framework. It floated nearer and then, as she brushed it with her finger-tips it bobbed away again . . . but at last she shouted:

"Tom, catch!"

"What is it?"

"Careful—it'll break."

She listened to hear if he caught it; then she stood up and looked around her for a way up.

"It's only a bottle," he called. Then: "Katie . . ."

"Yes?"

"There's something funny about it. It's sealed up and . . ."

"Yes?"

9

"Come on up quickly! There's something inside it!"

There was a sort of step up here, another there; with arms and legs stretching and twisting, she made her way up quite easily. Tom was waiting at the top, breathless with impatience.

"We'll have to break it open. Look!"

He held it up to show her. It was a wine bottle made of thick green glass with a full, rounded body and a long neck. It had been firmly corked, covered over with a large twist of metal foil and sealed with a broad band of red wax.

"Let me do it, I found it!"

But Tom was already smashing it with full force against the bollard; and it broke cleanly into four pieces. A tight roll of stiff, creamy paper, thick as parchment, dropped onto the ground between their feet.

"It's a message!" exclaimed Katie, picking it up gingerly.

The paper crackled satisfyingly at her touch. Tom pulled at it with eager fingers.

"Let's see what it says then."

The paper unfurled reluctantly to reveal a handwritten inscription in fading brown ink:

"The silver children of the sea
Swim blind towards a dreadful night.
Men too are blind with cruelty —
My beacon is their only light."

"It's gibberish," said Tom.

"It can't be," said Katie. "Why should anybody write gibberish and then take so much trouble to wrap it up like that and float it out to sea?"

"Then it must be a secret code," said Tom. "Something you have to unravel to find out what it really says."

"It must be something important," said Katie. "What do you think it means?"

"There should be a clue," said Tom. "A key-word. Else no one could even *begin* to understand it."

"It sounds a bit sinister, doesn't it?" said Katie. "'A dreadful night'... 'Blind with cruelty'..."

"Look at the last line though," said Tom thoughtfully. "'Beacon', 'light'—what's that make you think of?"

"Oh—I know—a lighthouse?"

"*The* lighthouse!"

"Tom," she said, "you don't think this has come from *there*?"

He nodded slowly and read out the verse again, whispering the final line as if it were a mystic incantation.

Little darts of panic began to stab at Katie's chest.

"So what if it *is* from the lighthouse?" she said quickly. "There's nothing..."

"We ought to go there," said Tom, "to find out."

"I'm not going anywhere near the place," said Katie. "It's not that I'm scared..."

"You are!"

". . . Not that I'm scared of the rocks. But you must have heard what they say about the Head Keeper. . ."

"You're a coward," said Tom blankly. "You said yourself this is important."

". . . You *know* he's meant to be a raving loony! If you want him to come swearing and chucking things after you, that's one adventure you can have on your own!"

The misty dampness of the afternoon grew oppressive, as if some dim, heavy question hung in the balance between them.

"Listen Kate," said Tom, rolling up the paper as he spoke, and then slowly unfurling it again.

"Be careful with that," she said.

"Kate," said Tom, "I was going to tell you something before you fell down that hole. . ."

"Before you pushed me down!"

". . . About the fish." He paused significantly. "You didn't happen to see any down there, did you?"

"No."

"Well, I don't think there are any fish left *anywhere*. None in the sea. *No fish at all.*"

She stared at him through the fine veil of rain.

"Whyever not?"

"It's my dad you see," Tom went on. "He suddenly seems to have stopped going to work. He always used to be out on the boats in the mornings before dawn and not back from unloading the fish till after dark—but now he just hangs around at home. I've been puzzling about it for ages; and then I began to wonder..."

"There could be a good reason for it ..."

"There isn't," said Tom. "I asked him."

"What did he say?"

"Nothing much. 'Fishing's bad', that's all, and then changed the subject quickly. I was wondering if this message..."

"Come to think of it," said Katie, "*my* dad's been having a lot of time off too. And my mum's been acting all moody and keeps going on about money."

"Something funny's going on," said Tom.

"All right then," said Katie, "supposing there really aren't any fish in the sea. They can't all have just disappeared. There must be an explanation. Let's see that message again."

She took the paper from him and stared at the curious, cryptic words. There was something about them....

"Tom," she said at last, "I think you're right. I bet it *is* from him. And it must have been sent for a reason. We ought to go to the Light and see him. And if he won't let us ashore, perhaps one of the other keepers might come down and tell us something."

"Can you be here tomorrow then," said Tom, "at the same time? What about a boat?"

"We'll ask at the harbour office," said Katie. "I expect old Angus will let us have one."

It was raining quite hard now. Tom folded the

paper carefully and put it in the inner pocket of his anorak.

"See you tomorrow then, Kate—and just one thing..."

"I know," she said, "we've got to keep it close. I won't tell anyone—cross my heart!"

2   The Lighthouse

"You want a boat then, do you?" said Angus
Dougall, blowing huge puffs of acrid pipe-smoke
into the air. "Well what sort will you be wanting?"

"Just a small one," said Tom. "Just for an hour or
two."

"And where'll you be going in it?"

"Not far," said Katie quickly.

"I had the trippers taking out the boats all
summer," said Angus, "with their binoculars and
transistor radios, saying they were going to do a
spot of fishing. But myself, I think it was them as
frightened all of the fish away."

He regarded them from under bushy eye-
brows.

"Have your fathers been laid up too?" he asked.

They nodded.

"It's bad, isn't it?" said Katie.

"It'll pass," said old Angus. "We've had bad
seasons before, though none like this, I'm bound to
admit. Now then, can you swim? Know about
currents and everything?"

They nodded again.

"You'll find oars in the bottom in case the motor

should fail. The *Clansman*, number 6 as you go down the quayside. Three hours only mind, and watch the rocks."

The *Clansman* was a wooden dinghy, with an outboard motor, a plastic bucket for bailing out and two long, yellow oars stacked neatly below the seat. They had to pull hard to get the rusty old engine going; but after several attempts it wheezed into life and soon they were speeding through the autumn sunshine out of the harbour and onto the open sea.

Behind them the whitewashed village quickly grew smaller until it was scarcely more than a thin, bright line against the gold and purple mountains. All around stretched the sea, a deep, inky wetness laced with swirling white where the restless waves rose and fell. The wind rushed through their hair and made the skin on their faces tingle; and their lips were soon coated with the salty taste of spray.

The little boat rode smoothly over the swell. Ahead, perhaps half a mile to the west, but steadily drawing nearer, lay a small archipelago of rocky islets dominated by the tall, white tower of the lighthouse.

"It'll be tricky landing," said Tom as they approached the first of the rocks. "Look at it!"

Powerful, frothing breakers were throwing themselves against the island, one after another, seeming to tear at the very foundations and casting up vast clouds of spray.

"Well they manage to get the other keepers on and off the relief boat somehow," said Katie doubtfully. She shaded her eyes to get a better view, but all she could make out was more rocks.

They slowed the engine to chug past the cliffs. The place looked barren and unwelcoming: a flock of gulls suddenly flew up at their approach, pale grey wings beating hard, yellow beaks screeching out a raucous warning. From all sides the lighthouse island seemed as impenetrable as a fortress.

"It's impossible," said Katie.

"It can't be," said Tom. "There *must* be a landing. Let's look again."

So round they went once more, hugging the cliffs as closely as they dared.

"Wait!" yelled Katie and she stopped the engine so abruptly that the boat ground to a standstill with a lop-sided jerk. Without its drone the roar of the wind and the surf was almost deafening. "Let's go back—I saw something! Don't bother about the engine, it's not far, we can row."

They each took an oar and began to pull with long, labouring strokes against the seaweed-laden waves.

"Come in a bit closer," shouted Katie. "Now—do you see?"

Right through the heart of the dark, forbidding crags, a deep chasm scored, as if the rock had cracked apart, forming a long corridor just wide enough to take a small boat. It was impossible to see what lay beyond because after a few yards there was a sharp corner.

"Looks like someone's private entrance," said Tom.

"Come on," said Katie, "it's the only way."

With barely enough room to swing the oars on either side of the boat, they rowed cautiously through the opening. All at once the noise of the sea and the wind was gone, as if it had been switched off.

An eerie silence enveloped them, broken only by the swishing of their oars against the water and a faint echo from the rock walls.

Above the gloom and the bare, damp walls hung the sky, very pale blue and patched with fluffy, wind-blown clouds. Ahead of them and over-shadowed by the looming rock face, the quiet channel of water glistened like a silvery-green snake.

Then they came to a dead end and a flight of rough, steep steps, hewn straight out of the cliff, loomed up in front of them.

"There must be almost a hundred," whispered Katie, "and they look as if they're meant for people with giant legs." She shuddered. "Perhaps we shouldn't be here."

"Well the keepers obviously get up and down them all right," said Tom. "Look, there's their boat."

He pointed to a low, cave-like recess at the bottom of the steps where a small, curiously-shaped boat with leather sides was moored.

They drew in the oars and rocked gently up and down. As they waited there uncertainly, from somewhere overhead there came a tapping—like footsteps, only broken and uneven.

They looked at each other and held their breath.

Then, loud and sudden as a thunderclap, a voice bellowed at them from the top of the steps:

"What are ye wanting? Keep away from my boat! Who asked ye here, snooping around when I've got a day and a night of work to do and more! Be off wi' ye now . . . go on, get away!"

They saw a small, wiry man with white hair, a white beard clipped close to his chin and a face that was as brown as a new conker. He was dressed in a navy blue uniform and a smart cap with a shiny, black peak was perched on the back of his head. In his right hand he carried a wooden walking-stick which he waved furiously at them.

"We've come to see you!" yelled Katie, as boldly as she dared. "We found your message!"

"What's that? Och, ye're children! Ye should know better than to come out here when the sea's up and stirring for a fight. What d'ye want?"

"I don't think he heard," whispered Tom. So they both shouted together: "We found your poem! We found your message in the bottle!" But he only shook his head at them and waved his stick more fiercely than ever.

"Supposing it's not from him after all?" whispered Katie.

"Let's try showing it to him," replied Tom. He took the thick, creamy roll of paper out of his pocket and waved it frantically at the Principal Keeper.

As soon as he saw what it was, a change came

over the man: he put down his stick and screwed up his eyes to peer at them. Then he began to climb down the long staircase, leaning heavily on a rope support and stepping awkwardly as if he had some difficulty in walking.

"What's that?" he asked sharply when at last he reached them. His eyes were very green and he had a disconcerting way of staring directly at them.

"We found this floating in a bottle," said Tom, adding, "sir," because he had a queer feeling that this meeting was very important and that they ought to get on the right side of the keeper if they possibly could. "It looks like a secret code, but we've tried to work it out and it seemed that it might have come from the lighthouse."

The man scrutinised them without a word until they were both blushing uncomfortably under his gaze. He was certainly a curious-looking fellow: they could not even guess how old he was, for his hair, which from a distance had looked completely white, was in fact a pale yellow streaked with grey; and the wrinkles on his face might have been caused either by old age or merely by the wind and sun.

"Where are ye from?" he said at last. Before they could reply, he added, as if greedy to know: "When did ye find it? And how did ye know it was mine?"

"We found it in the harbour, sir," said Katie, meeting his stare for a moment. "We guessed you might have sent it by the bit about the beacon and we thought maybe... well we thought we *ought* to come."

"'Tis only a wee bit of poetry," said the Lighthouse Keeper. "I wrote it five or six weeks ago, when my heart was starting to break. And I threw it to the selchies, for 'tis for them that I wrote it. Never for once dreaming 'twould be found by children." A dreamy glaze came into his eyes; but suddenly he turned sharply to them again. "However, since ye've come, I had best take it as an omen to be acted upon. Throw me a rope now and come ashore!"

He tied their boat up next to his own leather one and they followed him up the steps. Each one was as wide as it was long and the height between them was so great that they could only make slow progress, one foot at a time. Moreover the Keeper was hindered by his limp, though they were more out of breath than he was by the time they reached the top.

To their surprise, the jagged-edged plateau on top of the cliffs was completely covered with grass, and there was even a little patch of garden fenced in around the low outbuildings of the lighthouse, full of rows and rows of cabbages and potatoes. A strong, eye-watering wind straight off the sea hit them as they left the shelter of the chasm.

Without a word the Keeper led them to an iron ladder propped against the circular wall of the lighthouse, and up this to the front door which stood wide open. He banged it loudly shut behind them so that the sudden warmth and quietness took them by surprise.

They found themselves in a circular, thick-walled chamber of un-plastered brick; it seemed to be a kind of store, for it was full of piles of ropes, oil-cans, lanterns, thigh-high waders, various metal implements and tools, several buckets and three sets of yellow oilskin overalls. It smelt strongly of paraffin and the sea.

They did not stop here, however, but hurried across to a tightly spiralling stone staircase in the opposite wall which led up through a hole in the ceiling.

The next room contained many greasy engines and polished brass instruments and echoed with the low hum of a generator. Two men were hard at work in there with scrubbing brushes and a tin of polish. They looked up in astonishment as Tom and Katie entered. But the Principal Keeper only muttered at them: "Get on wi' it, laddies, and mind your own business!" before leading Tom and Katie on up the well-swept, winding stairway.

There was more machinery on the next level too.

Then at last they reached the fourth floor and entered what clearly were the living quarters.

As soon as they were all inside, the Keeper snapped a heavy door shut over the staircase, shot a bolt across and bade them both sit down.

3   The Sorrow of the Selchies

The Keepers' parlour was, like the whole lighthouse completely round. There were four small, double-paned windows equally spaced high up around the thick wall and these too were round and opened inwards, like portholes on a ship.

Three wooden chairs stood around a well-scrubbed table in the centre of the concrete floor. A kettle was singing softly on an old-fashioned kitchen range under one of the windows; there was also an enamel sink and a tall cabinet containing three lockers. There was no other furniture.

Everything was neat and gleaming clean, as if the occupants spent much of their time keeping the place shipshape; even the blue and white paint which adorned everything looked fresh.

"Now then, now then," said the Principal Keeper stiffly when he had them both seated at the table. "I had better have your names please."

They told him.

"Myself, I am known as the Captain," he said. "'Tis the only name I have now. I lost my others many, many years ago; och yes, I lost them to the selchies in the sea."

"What are selchies?" asked Tom.

But the Captain did not answer; instead he said, "I have been hearing rumours, I have been hearing tales. They say there is trouble on the mainland—strange goings-on. Tell me, is it true? But whatever it is, surely there can be nothing so strange as what I have already seen out here amongst the waves."

"Well yes," said Tom, "there *is* something funny going on at home. The men are all laid off; and the whole village is sort of falling asleep...as if...almost as if someone had put an evil spell on the place!"

The Captain shot them a curious glance.

"The fish have all disappeared you see," said Katie.

At that the Captain leaped up, banging the table with his fist.

"Och!" he exclaimed, "so that is what it is all about! But now tell me this: *who are they blaming it on*, my friends?"

He went over to his locker and pulled out various tins and utensils from the neat stack inside. "Ye'll have some cocoa with me?"

"Yes please," said Tom.

"Blame it on?" said Katie. "What do you mean?"

"Why, I mean that soon they will be blaming it on the selchies!" said the Captain excitedly, mixing up some instant milk and putting it in a saucepan to heat on top of the stove. "Ye can be sure of that! Och, it does make my very heart bleed to think of what sorrow will be coming to them."

"Hold on," said Tom, "you still haven't told us: what *are* the selchies?"

The Captain turned to them with a look that was half-way between horror and amazement on his nut-brown face.

"Are ye telling me," he said, "as true as an oath, that ye do not know the selchies?"

They shook their heads in shame at their ignorance.

"'Tis *who* are they, ye should be asking," cried the Captain, his eyes flashing angrily at them. "Is there no respect left in this world? 'Tis no wonder things take such a turn!" He handed them thick, dark cocoa in enamel mugs.

"Selchie," he went on, but more gently now, "why, that is the old name for the grey Atlantic seal. Och, but 'seal' is only a half-name, for the selchies are more—far more—than wee ignorant beasties."

He sat down again and shook his head sadly, staring into his cocoa.

"Now then, since ye appear to learn nothing of the old wisdom at school, it is best that I should be telling ye something about it. So will ye hark at this. It is said that when a man is drowned at sea, his soul is not lost, but that it goes for evermore into the care and safe-keeping of the selchies. And then too, there are those who will tell ye that at certain phases of the moon, the selchies do come upon the land to shed their skins and dance beneath the stars in the shape of fair earth-maidens; though at first light they will return in their seal-skins to the sea."

At first Katie and Tom were so afraid of laughing that they did not dare to look at each other. But the Captain seemed quite serious and his manner was so urgent, that soon they began to listen more carefully.

"There are many, many strange stories that I have heard long ago from the old folk of the lonely islands far to the north and the west. They told me tales of miraculous deeds upon the sea when the selchies mixed their fate with that of humankind, and they taught me the many signs and omens by which it is possible to tell when a child has the selchie-blood running in his veins. But of course, there is no way of knowing whether any of this is true."

His voice faltered, as if he had something more to say about which he hesitated.

"What did you mean," Tom prompted him, "when you said you lost your name to the selchies?"

"I have a gammy leg," replied the Captain gruffly. "D'ye see it?"

They nodded, embarrassed.

"If 'twere not for the selchies, I would have no leg at all: I would be nothing but a heap of old white bones at the bottom of the sea."

He watched them carefully from narrowed eyes as he spoke, as if anxious to observe exactly how they reacted to his story.

"'Twas in the mad, black days of the war," he

went on, "when I was as crazy as the rest. We were flying over the sea one winter's night looking for enemy ships to bomb. But they spotted our plane first and fired at us...then I remember a great explosion, pain shooting through my leg...and after that a void. I found myself all alone in the icy sea and by all logic and natural law, I should have frozen within minutes and then drowned."

The round, blue-and-white room seemed very still as he spoke. Outside they could hear the wind buffeting against the thick walls of the tower.

Katie asked gently: "Did the seals save you?"

He nodded. "I was not afraid, because in the darkness I heard singing."

"Singing?"

"Aye. 'Twas not the angels, nor was it simply the music of the sea; because then I saw the selchies."

He paused and they listened to the pounding of the waves far below; from within the tower, the low, regular hum of the generator, and a clock ticking quietly on the wall above the door.

"The selchies were singing the sweetest, saddest song that ever I have heard," he said. "All I remember is their singing and their warm bodies swimming behind me in the cold night and their soft deep eyes turned upon me.

"And then I awoke, safe and alive in sheets of white linen. I never learned in full how I came to safety; aye, but I shall never forget that night out on the winter sea, all alone with the selchies."

He took a long draught from his mug and then,

shaking his head, smiled sadly and secretly to himself.

"Since then," he said, "I have been wary of the company of others; they think me odd and aloof. I keep myself apart here on this island as much as I can; I never take my leave ashore, for it could be no pleasure to me. But the selchies are different. Aye, the selchies are my true and only friends."

"But what about your message," asked Tom, "and all this talk of 'trouble'?"

"Trouble!" exclaimed the Captain, suddenly roused again, his eyes flashing with anger. "Yes indeed, I will tell ye about trouble! They are after the selchies' skins and they are rogues who will stop at nothing! Villains, the very devils they are!"

"But who?" asked Katie, "and what do..." But the Captain's penetrating stare cut her off in mid-sentence. She blushed and faltered, "Oh, I'm sorry... we're asking so many questions."

"Ask what ye will," replied the Captain. "Ye are of no use to me at all unless ye know fully what is in the wind. So I shall tell ye about the fearful noises that come across the ocean in the dead of night so that it would make your very soul tremble to hear them; and I have often seen a dark ship with not a light on board go sailing by on the furthest line of the horizon where it has no business to be."

"Why would it do that?" asked Tom.

The Captain shook his head and drummed restlessly with his finger-tips upon the table.

"I have my ideas; but 'tis the selchies themselves

who could best tell ye, for I do believe they have the second sight."

He rose from his chair and went across to one of the high, round windows from which he gazed longingly out to the rocky islets scattered amongst the distant waves.

"'Tis almost October and they should be coming ashore now for the breeding season. But where are they? I have seen them swimming all around here, they have come again from the further reaches of the ocean; but why will they not come on to the land? The bulls are thin and the cows have the sadness of the very Deep within their eyes; and I think that they are afraid."

He turned back to them and now his eyes were gleaming.

"Will ye help me, my friends?"

Tom said "yes" at once; but Katie hesitated.

"I think so," she said. "What do you want us to do?"

"I can see my talk is strange to ye," said the Captain, "but this is a serious business." He sat down again, taking off his cap and leaning earnestly across the table towards them.

"Ye must listen. Ye must watch. Soon upon the mainland ye will hear talk of the selchies. Ye will hear more talk about the disappearing fish. And...maybe there will be other words whispered too: about a disease—a plague—upon the sea."

Again, the sad shaking of his white head as if he knew more than he would say.

"We'll look for clues," said Tom, "and we'll come straight back—as soon as we can borrow a boat—and let you know if we find out anything."

"I think there *is* something going on," said Katie, trying hard to remember. "I've seen strangers in the village—they start to talk about the fish and then suddenly they stop, as if there was something to hide."

A tap at the door made them all jump: it was still bolted.

The Captain made no move to open it; instead he replaced his cap, glanced at the clock and drew himself stiffly to attention.

"Yes?" he barked.

A man's voice from outside began, "Captain, my watch is finished . . ."

"Yes, yes, I know," snapped the Captain. "I am taking over now. Be gone and leave me in peace!"

Suddenly now he was brisk and efficient: he brushed away his memories and visions like cobwebs.

"It is almost sunset," he said. "In five minutes I must light my beacon." He led them to the door and shook them each by the hand. "Will ye be going now?"

It was more of a command than a question and, before they could answer, he had already released the bolt, opened the door and was rapidly descending the twisting stone staircase to the lower rooms, with scarcely a backward glance to see if they were following. There was no sign of either of his assistants and their steps echoed emptily through the tall cavity of the tower.

"Ye will find your way safely back across the sea?" he asked as he led them out across the windy island, back to the top of the hundred rocky steps; but before they could answer he had left them and was hurrying back to his lighthouse.

By the time they had clambered back into their boat he had already lit the beacon, and the yellow, comforting light was flashing for twenty miles all around over the sea.

4   "Kill the Seals!"

Screeching their brakes and honking impatiently
spattering up mud and gravel, a steady stream of
battered cars made their way through the sprawling
streets of the village and drew up in front of the
grey stone hall in the little central square. Crowds
of other people came walking and running down
the hill towards the hall, until the whole area in
front of its open doors was filled with a loudly
gossiping throng.

At first glance it might have been Christmas or
some special local fête; yet there was no sign of any
merriment amongst all the headscarfed women and
moodily smoking men who were gathering there in
the dusk.

Katie and Tom were there too: one by one they
threaded their way through the crowd to meet, as
they had agreed, under the yellow notice that was
pinned to the board of the village hall.

FISHING CRISIS
Important Meeting,
Village Hall, Saturday.
A guest speaker will address the village.
All are strongly urged to attend.

"I've brought a notebook," said Katie as the burly local constable ushered everyone into the brightly-lit hall. "We don't want to forget anything that we ought to tell the Captain."

They found a seat on the end of the back row of hard, wobbly chairs, next to two fat women.

Tom gazed round at the grim-faced, muttering assembly. "I wonder who this guest speaker is, and whether he's got anything useful to say."

"By the looks of everyone he'd better come up with something pretty strong," said Katie. She opened her notebook importantly and took a new, blue pencil out of her pocket.

"My dad's hoping for some action," said Tom. He says we shouldn't all sit around just accepting things any longer and that somebody or something must be to blame."

There was a great deal of scraping of chairs and coughing and fidgeting; and then old Angus Dougall climbed up onto the rostrum to open the meeting.

"Friends," he began, "we are facing a most strange and troublesome phenomenon in our local waters. Something has happened to our fish! We've hit hard times and, though we're all sticking together as we always have done, the strain's beginning to tell."

There were grunts of "aye!" and "hear hear!" from around the room.

"As yet," continued old Angus, scratching his ear and looking nervous, "no one's come up with any explanation or solution. But the outside world has not forgotten us, my friends. Yesterday morning I was telephoned from London by a gentleman who says he may be able to help us. He drove up today and arrived just half an hour ago. It's the first glimmer of hope that we've had and, although he's a stranger to these parts, I hope you'll all make him welcome."

He cleared his throat.

"Mr Edward da Silva is his name. He's a learned man—a Master of Science, so he tells me. He's also Managing Director of a company called Silva Enterprises Ltd. I'll leave it to him to explain what he can do for us."

Old Angus gave a self-conscious little bow and hurried down the steps. There was some polite clapping and then an elegant young man stood up and took his place on the platform.

He was tall and straight with sleek, dark hair, a polished complexion and a thick, carefully-trimmed moustache. He wore a well-tailored suit and a deep-coloured silk tie; upon the little finger of his left hand was a gold ring, prominently set with a square black stone.

"Ladies and gentlemen," he announced, "you have no fish and you want to know why."

His voice was as rich and smooth as his tie; he sounded as if he were addressing a gathering of princes rather than of fisherfolk and at first a titter ran round the room.

"There is plenty of fish down south. There is

plenty of fish on the east coast. But suddenly there is none here in the North-West, here where you noble people have lived and earned your living from the sea for generations. But you will be pleased to hear that there is a simple explanation—and therefore a simple solution."

"Get on with it!" shouted a rough voice from the back.

Katie stopped doodling in her notebook and held her pencil ready to write down what he was about to say.

"Ladies and gentlemen, there is a pestilence upon your seas. You are the victims of a plague—a plague of seals."

There was not a sound from anyone in the warm, crowded hall. Edward da Silva looked boldly around, watching his words sink in and observing the stunned silence with satisfaction.

"The seals have eaten all your fish."

"Oh Tom," whispered Katie, "it's just what the Captain said! He's blaming the selchies!"

"Let me enlarge," said Mr da Silva, unrolling a large chart on which was drawn a complicated graph with the title *Grey Seal Fertility and Multiplication*. "The seal population on the rocks off your coast has increased five-fold in the last ten years. I know this because Silva Enterprises has recently carried out this careful survey and statistical count on behalf of a naturalists' organisation. The facts quite clearly speak for themselves. If there are five times as many seals they must be eating five times as many fish. Sooner or later they will have eaten all the fish that there are."

An angry murmur ran round the room. Tom and Katie could see Mr da Silva measuring it, sensing that feeling was running high; and now he whipped it up.

"Ladies and gentlemen, you must destroy the surplus numbers! You must kill them! You must organise a cull! The seals are vermin! They are eating all your fish!"

Out of the growing hubbub a man's voice called, "How many are ye thinking we should kill?"

Mr da Silva smoothed down an imaginary stray strand of hair. "I suggest we eliminate four fifths of them," he said, "to bring us back to the manageable numbers of ten years ago." He gave a dry, forced laugh. "After all, there is no reason why we should not allow just a few of them to live, now is there?"

By now, the very air was tingling with excited shouts of, "Kill them! Kill the seals!"; but an old man's voice cut across the others:

"'Tis a wicked thing you're suggesting! We've always shared the sea with the selchies. 'Tis bad luck to go doing them harm!"

"Nonsense!" retorted a woman, "there's children will be starving if we don't do something soon. What could be worse luck than that?"

Mr da Silva looked smug and knowledgeable.

"It's not so long ago," he reminded them, "that many people throughout the coasts of northern Europe made their living through sealing. Good grief, ladies and gentlemen, nobody worried about silly superstitions then! They needed the meat to eat and the blubber for oil-lamps and the skins for boots, so out they went and caught them. And of course in those days there was always plenty of fish for everyone."

"I'm not schooled like ye are sir," said the old man, "and I'll not vouch for the rest of Europe. But the folks round here have always minded the selchies. Why, I've known families who'd go barefoot rather than touch . . ."

But scores of others were shouting him down: "Aw, be quiet Grandad, this is the twentieth century!" "We need our living and we need our fish!" "Let the speaker finish!"

"It's bad, Tom," said Katie.

"Awful," said Tom. "Have you got it all down? His name and everything?"

"Ssshh," said Katie, "look, old Angus is getting up again."

"Mr da Silva," said Angus, "I believe that you may be able to help us with this, er, cull that you're proposing?"

Edward da Silva smiled diffidently. "My dear sir," he said, "I hate to presume . . . but if I could possibly be of any service . . . Silva Enterprises have what you might call quite considerable experience in this kind of operation. We would be delighted to provide weapons and ammunition and to organise you good people into a shooting party. It should only take a day or two and we would dispose of the bodies at no inconvenience to yourselves."

"That sounds most impressive," said Angus. "When do you think you could start?"

"We must get them while they're breeding you see," said Mr da Silva, looking quite excited at the prospect. "Kill the pups as soon as they're born, as well as the adults. We must cut off the evil at the root! If they follow the usual patterns, they'll be coming ashore to give birth within the next couple of weeks—that's the time to catch them! So would it suit you if we start two weeks from now, ladies and gentlemen?" He smiled apologetically. "I'm so sorry that it's not practical to begin sooner."

"So *that's* why the Captain noticed the selchies aren't coming ashore," whispered Tom. "Somehow they must know. But it can't be true that they're taking the fish—it can't be!"

"Well we've got two weeks to stop them," said Katie, "and that's hardly any time at all."

"Friends," said Angus Dougall, "let's decide together on our course of action. A seal cull's not a pleasant thing; but our livelihood's at stake. Let's have a vote on it. Will all those in favour of the cull show their hands?"

A great sea of hands rose and the angry murmurs grew to a deafening roar: "Get rid of the vermin!" "Let's have our fish back!" "Kill them, the sooner the better!" "Kill the seals!"

Old Angus waved them all down.

"I'm delighted to see we are all acting together," he said. "Well friends, I'll make arrangements for

Silva Enterprises to help us on the Saturday after next. Now, before we all go home, has anyone got any more questions or comments?"

"I have a question." A tall, middle-aged woman with thick steel-grey hair, stood up in the centre of the room. Her voice rang clear and strong as a bell across the hall. "I should like to ask Mr Edward da Silva how he can prove that the seals have really increased at such an alarmingly unlikely rate and that they are really responsible for the sudden disappearance of the fish?"

"Listen Kate," whispered Tom, "she might be on our side."

Edward da Silva flashed his white teeth in a charming smile beneath his dapper moustache. "Madam," he said, "I am so glad you have asked this. The figures gathered by Silva Enterprises for our wild-life survey are freely available to the public. As I said, the facts speak for themselves. I shall gladly send you a copy if you would like to give me your name and address..."

"Mr da Silva," boomed the woman, drawing herself up to her full stature, "I shall study these figures of yours very carefully. I have reason to, shall we say, dispute them. To put it bluntly, I disagree with you most strongly, Mr da Silva. I think you are talking dangerous nonsense. Your proposal is both foolish and wicked."

For the first time, Edward da Silva looked taken aback: he even seemed to be blushing. Still, his voice remained smooth and calm.

"I'm so sorry that you don't understand me, Madam," he said. "If you'd just like to give me your name . . ."

"I understand you perfectly," she interrupted him, "and I am quite sure you are wrong in every way. My name is Hermione Northcote-McPherson, since you seem so anxious to know it. And I have little doubt, Mr da Silva, that you and I are going to have quite a bit to say to each other before the next fortnight is out."

5   Mrs Northcote-McPherson

"We'll have to go and see her," said Tom, "and then report back to the Captain."

"But she's an old dragon!" said Katie. "You saw her—and heard her. I'm sure she'd never listen to us."

"But we've *got* to," insisted Tom. "She's on the same side as us. Everyone else has gone mad!"

"I know," said Katie, "my dad voted for the cull and my mun. And so did yours."

"My dad's getting desperate," said Tom. "He says if things don't look up in a few weeks we'll have to leave. Go somewhere else. He says he won't sit back any longer accepting things. That's how they all feel, Kate. But I saw a programme about a seal cull in Canada on the telly once: the poor things don't stand a chance. They shoot them at point blank range and club the pups to death in full view of their mothers—really brutal it is."

"But the thing is," said Katie slowly, twisting a strand of hair round and round her fingers and then untwisting it again, "supposing Mr da Silva is *right* and the seals really are to blame?"

Tom opened his mouth to disagree, but she went

on: "I mean *something's* happened to the fish, hasn't it? And why should the crazy old Captain know any more what's right than him?"

"I know what you're getting at," said Tom, "but it still comes back to Mrs Northcote-McPherson. Everyone knows she's written dozens of books on natural history and you can't say she doesn't know what she's talking about. I still think we ought to tell her about the Captain; and then we ought to go and tell the Captain all about her."

Hermione Northcote-McPherson lived in a large, Victorian, greystone house at the bottom of a hill half a mile outside the village. It was set back from the main road in a large garden full of trees: huge, ancient oaks and chestnuts and, in one corner, an orchard of apple trees and plums.

They turned through a pair of heavy, iron gates and up the drive. Dusk was falling and a light breeze rustled the trees, causing a shower of yellow and brown leaves that seemed strangely vivid in the half-light. More leaves were piled in huge drifts along the edge of the sweeping lawns and they could smell a bonfire smoking.

Soft lights shone through two curtained windows on the ground floor and a carriage lamp burned over the porch.

There was no doorbell: instead they found a heavy brass knocker shaped like a dolphin that resounded with an echoing thud when Tom lifted it, and let it drop.

Almost at once they heard footsteps; then the front door swung open and they stood face to face with Mrs Northcote-McPherson.

For a few moments the noble lady stared down at them in utter surprise; but then her stern features broke into a smile.

"Well, good evening to you," she said. "No doubt you have called for a purpose? What can I do for you?"

Despite everything there was something homely about her: perhaps it was because she smiled so broadly that she revealed unexpected toothless gaps; or because her clothes—tweed skirt, cashmere cardigan, sheepskin slippers and even the string of pearls around her throat—all looked old and well-worn and comfortable. Maybe she was not such a dragon after all.

Katie took a deep breath and tried hard not to go red.

"I hope you don't mind us coming to see you like this," she said, "but there's something ever so important that we'd like to talk to you about."

"It's about the selchies," said Tom. "The seals. We heard you speak at the meeting and we agree with you because ... well, we've heard some strange things to do with the fish that we thought we ought to tell you."

"Aha!" exclaimed Mrs Northcote-McPherson, "have you now? I shall be mighty glad to listen if you can suggest anything that could help me in my campaign. I must confess I was beginning to think the whole village had gone utterly idiotic! Thank goodness at least you two seem to have your heads screwed on the right way round! Why, you'd better come in—yes, come in, come in!"

She led them down a short, dark corridor and through an oak door that creaked on its hinges, into a room that was warm and bright with a log fire. Several large, battered, chintz-covered chairs were grouped around the hearth and there was a general clutter of books, trailing plants and outlandish wooden carvings. A strong smell of lavender wafted over from a large bowl of dried flowers which stood on the mantelpiece.

Above this hung a huge oil painting of an eccentric-looking Edwardian gentleman with great, bushy side-whiskers. There were also many other, smaller pictures all over the faded walls: framed sketches in pen-and-ink or water-colours of curious exotic birds, reptiles and flowers.

"Now then," said Mrs Northcote-McPherson, "what would you like? Tea? Crumpets?"

They half expected her to ring for a servant; but instead she bustled out herself, returning shortly with a large tray on which stood a bone-china tea-service, a steaming, silver teapot, a dish of yellow, creamy butter and a large plate heaped high with crumpets.

"Make yourselves comfy!" she cried. "Why, you're as stiff as two brass monkeys, the pair of you! My goodness, don't mind *me*! Now, you'll have to toast the crumpets yourselves, if you don't mind. Look, there's a toasting-fork in the corner."

So while Tom knelt on the sheepskin rug, toasting one crumpet after another in front of the fire, Mrs Northcote-McPherson fired questions at them.

"Let's see, you'd better introduce yourselves first," she said thoughtfully, pouring tea into the cups with a noisy flourish.

"I'm Tom," said Tom.

"I'm Katie," said Katie.

"Thomas and Katherine," said Mrs Northcote-McPherson firmly. "I can't abide these silly nicknames. Now then, what have you got to tell me?"

"Well, it's about the seals, as we said," began Katie. "You see, last week Tom and I went out to the lighthouse and we got talking to the Principal Keeper."

"Good gracious child, you didn't! They say the man's as mad as a hatter! Did he really let you ashore?"

"Oh yes," said Tom, "when he discovered why we'd come. Because we found this message in a bottle and it turned out to be him who'd sent it. He took us right up into the tower and then he told us some really weird stories. At first we didn't know what to make of them at all . . . until we started to tie them up with all the things that have been happening — and especially with what was said at the meeting."

"Go on," said Mrs Northcote-McPherson.

"He was talking about the seals, you see. Only he called them selchies. And he said that something was wrong with them. And then he kept asking us if there was trouble at home and if we'd heard anything about the seals."

"He's quite bonkers," said Katie, spreading butter on a crumpet and giving Tom another to fit onto the end of his toasting-fork. "But—well, not *quite*. I mean, he can't be, can he, if he's in charge of the lighthouse. But honestly, the things he told us! About funny noises he hears in the dead of night. And a big, dark ship he keeps seeing with no lights on board at all."

Mrs Northcote-McPherson looked up sharply and fixed Katie with a penetrating gaze. "What else, child?" she said.

"It was all a bit of a muddle," Katie went on. "Sort of garbled. We had to ask him lots of times before he'd explain what he meant by selchies and then he kept telling us soppy fairy tales about them—trying to make out that seals are half-human and that sort of thing.

"Yes, yes," interrupted Mrs Northcote-McPherson impatiently. "That's nothing new—the selchie legends used to be well known around here when I was a child. But tell me more about these noises. And the dark ship."

"He didn't really say much, except that he'd seen and heard them," said Tom. "But he was ever so interested in the fish disappearing and then he started going on about the seals behaving strangely and, the thing is, since we heard Mr da Silva saying they should all be killed, a lot of what the Captain told us seems to tie in."

"I should most certainly think it does," said Mrs Northcote-McPherson, pouring them each a second cup of tea. "You must bring this keeper fellow to see me. As soon as possible."

"Oh," exclaimed Katie, "but I'm sure he won't want to come!"

Mrs Northcote-McPherson stood up, puffing herself out like one of the tropical birds in her pictures.

"Whatever do you mean?" she demanded. "Of course he must come! I shall write him a formal invitation and perhaps you two children will be good enough to deliver it to him for me."

She went over to a polished, mahogany writing bureau that stood in a corner of the room. From its neat pigeon-holes she took up thick paper and a silver fountain pen and scribbled a brief note in large, sweeping handwriting.

She sealed the letter carefully inside a blue envelope and gave it to Katie.

"Urgent business," she said.

"Do you think we can stop the cull?" asked Tom as they got up to go.

"We must," said Mrs Northcote-McPherson. "We've got to. He's a villain, this da Silva chappie. This is only the first phase of his scheme, you can be sure of that. If we let them win, you wait and see — they'll be back next year on another part of the coast. The so-called 'seal-plague' will spread like wild-fire once it gets a hold. There'll be fishing famines throughout the land—and before you know it, the seals will all be gone. Extinct. The people fooled. And you can be sure that a certain gentleman stands to make a great deal of money out of it."

"But who are they?" asked Tom.

"They? Edward da Silva? Silva Enterprises? I'm not sure yet. But I have been putting two and two together—oh yes, I most certainly have my suspicions. And it sounds to me as if your Captain friend may have even more."

"You don't think that there's any chance that Mr da Silva might be right then?" asked Katie slowly. "I mean, it's all very well feeling sorry for the seals, but supposing they really *are* eating up all the fish?"

Mrs Northcote-McPherson retorted with a snort of a laugh.

"Pshaw girl!" she cried, "you're as half-witted as the rest of them! Why, your brains are as soft as fish-roes! Don't they teach you simple mathematics at school, eh? Biology? How could the seals possibly have multiplied five times in ten years? They're not rats or rabbits. Why, they only have one pup, once a year, and of those that survive the hazards of the rocks it takes them at least five years until they're old enough to start breeding themselves. I couldn't believe my very own ears and eyes when I saw all those people taken in!"

"Well, what *is* happening to the fish then?" asked

Katie, flushing.

"I'll tell you one thing," said Mrs Northcote-
McPherson, shooing them out into the dim
passageway and opening the front door to let in the
damp, bitter-sweet scent of an early autumn night.
"It's nothing to do with the seals. Poor, dumb
creatures—they take what they need and no more.
No, there are certain persons at the bottom of this."

She came out and stood on the porch, hands on
hips, gazing up at the star-embroidered sky and
shaking her head.

"People now. Yes, you can be sure that whatever
form trouble takes, whether it's on land or out at
sea, there are bound to be people to blame,
somewhere along the line."

6   A Summons from the Deep

There was so little time to lose that Tom and Katie
agreed they must pay a second visit to the
lighthouse as soon as school was over the following
afternoon.

Of course, the whole village was buzzing with
discussions about the cull and when they went into
old Angus Dougall's hut to see about taking the
boat out again, they found it crowded with his
cronies, all speculating about the coming event.

"...Got myself an old sealing net," said an
elderly, grey-jowled fisherman as they pushed open
the door. He rubbed thin, strong hands together.
"'Twas my grandaddy's. He used to go sealing by
nights you know, in his spare time. And a fine old
living he might have made of it, if he hadn't had to
keep it secret because the laird did not approve."

"Quite right!" cried another; and they recognised
the voice of the old man who had spoken up against
the cull at the meeting. "I only wish that ye would
all admit that it is bad luck to touch or to harm the
selchies. There's not a town or village up and down
this whole coast, aye, on the islands too, where
ye'll not find folk who would tell ye that!"

"That is nought but old wives' nonsense!" declared Angus Dougall. Katie coughed loudly and tried to catch his eye; but the harbour master seemed not to have noticed them. Instead, he began busily to poke out his pipe, spilling grimy tobacco over the open pages of his record book in which were written all the details of the local boats and their catches.

"But it's guns we'll be needing, not nets," he went on. "Let's get 'em sharp, let's get 'em quick boys—aye, and God help us, let's have our fish back, and our living too!"

It was quite hopeless trying to attract his attention, so Tom shouted out: "Mr Dougall! Can we borrow one of your boats again please?"

Silence fell, and a dozen eyes turned to stare at them. Tom swallowed.

"Would it be all right to take the *Clansman*?" he asked.

Old Angus smiled kindly at them. "Aye, ye may take her. But watch the sky now. The weather may be turning for the worst this evening."

"Never mind the weather—'tis the seals ye should be watching!" cried the fellow with the sealing net. He laughed drily. "They're maybe feeling so hungry, they'll be getting tired of fish and turning to eating children next!"

This caused a loud guffaw from all the others; so it was with some relief that Tom and Katie pushed their way out of the hut and ran down to the quay.

Despite old Angus's warning about the weather,

the day seemed fine enough; indeed the air was completely still, and the sea was even subdued and glassy when they reached the craggy rocks of the lighthouse island.

They sailed easily enough this time through the hidden inlet to the landing-stage, secured the boat and started up the hundred steps. But before they were even half-way up they stopped, because there was the wiry figure of the Captain perched at the top, regarding them solemnly through a long, brass telescope.

He came hurrying down to them in a lop-sided way because of his limp, looking not in the least surprised to see them.

"Och, and there ye are at last now!" he exclaimed. "Well, there is no point at all in tying up your boat—mine will not take three, and we might just as well be going straightaway."

"Where to?" asked Katie.

"Why, have ye not come to see how they are keeping and whether they are coming out yet from the sea? By all that is good, now is the time they should be having their wee, white babies."

"Do you mean the selchies?"

"And who else would I be talking about?" cried the Captain, looking quite exasperated at their hesitation. He hobbled down the last few steps and, without waiting for an invitation, stepped into their boat and began to untie it from its mooring.

"Hold on!" cried Tom as they leaped in hastily beside him, "that's just what we've come to see you about. They're in terrible danger, Captain!"

"Indeed, what was coming has come then," replied the Captain calmly, starting up the grimy old engine with no effort at all. "But such news cannot be any worse than what I have always feared, so it must wait a wee while longer." He pulled from his pocket a woollen hat that looked almost as old as he was and squashed it firmly down over his white hair. "Now, follow my directions please, and let us save the talking until our return."

They cruised round to the seaward side of the lighthouse island and straight past its immediate neighbours. At first they both wondered with some nervousness if he were steering an aimless path out to the open sea. But the Captain sat in the bows, smiling serenely as if he were still hearing the ancient selchie-music and gazing round at the ocean with the contented pride of a landlord reviewing his estate; and before long they saw that they were approaching another group of even smaller rocky islets.

Just then, Tom started up so suddenly that he almost tipped the boat over.

"Hey look!" he exclaimed, "there's somebody swimming over there!"

He pointed disbelievingly to a spot not far from the nearest rock. Sure enough, a plump face stared back at them, bobbing up and down in the cold water.

"Wherever can he have come from?" said Katie. "There are no other boats around and surely no one would have swum all the way out here—especially at this time of year. He looks so calm, almost as if he's just floating...oh," she shuddered, "*drowned people float, don't they?*"

But just then the head made a sudden dive and disappeared beneath the waves.

The Captain chuckled.

"Now are ye understanding?" he said. "The selchies are not like other beasties." He leaned towards them with a confidential manner. "They have the look about them of humans, their eyes are those of ones who have a soul."

Even as he spoke, two more seal heads popped up within a few yards of the boat, so that they could clearly see their whiskers and black, wet noses. Yet there was something disturbingly human about the smooth, round heads that glistened wet from the sea; and the warm, melting darkness of their eyes.

"We are coming close to one of their breeding spots," explained the Captain. "They are watching us, bless them, to see what we are about to do."

They sailed nearer and nearer to the skerries and now they could see that the whole stony archipelago was covered with seals. Their mottled coats—brown, grey and tawny—matched the colour of the seaweed-covered rocks so exactly that at first it was quite difficult to make them out; though small patches of creamy-white showed up where the first, day-old pups lay. Some were quite still, whilst others were wriggling about slowly and clumsily like huge caterpillars, and with none of the streamlined grace they displayed in the sea.

"There's thousands of them," cried Katie, scarcely able to believe her eyes, "millions! I never knew there were so many!"

"Ye will not often see them like this," said the Captain. "They are not landlubbers like us: mostly they are happiest out in the loneliest reaches of the wide ocean, where there is infinite space to keep them all."

He turned off the engine and let the boat drift. A quavery hooting, laced with broken, infantile snarls, came loud and mournful across the water from the rocks.

"Captain," said Tom suddenly, "we've *got* to tell you, now that we've seen them. They're going to shoot the selchies! The week after next!"

The keeper turned abruptly to look at him, wrinkling his eyes against the glare.

"Who?" he asked sharply. "Who will shoot my friends?" There was a slight tremor in his voice and his brown face paled.

"Silva Enterprises, that's who," said Katie. "You were right, Captain, there *has* been trouble at home. Everyone's saying that there are far too many seals, and that's why ..."

The Captain burst out: "I have read it in your eyes lassie: ye believe that too!"

"I do *not*!" declared Katie, "of course I don't, only ..." confusion overwhelmed her "... I didn't realise there were so many of them ... I mean—they must eat a lot of fish, mustn't they?"

"They are late this year," said the Captain, speaking as slowly and deliberately as if he were addressing a very young and rather foolish child. "That is because they are hungry. I will tell ye this: there is not enough fish for the selchies either. Indeed, it has all disappeared; and you can be sure that the selchies are blaming it upon the people, just as the people are blaming it upon the selchies."

"But they're going to kill the selchies, whoever's fault it is," cried Tom. "That's why we've brought you a letter—a very important one—from Mrs Northcote-McPherson."

"A letter!" exclaimed the Captain, as if such a thing had never happened to him before. "Who is this that has been writing to me?"

"Oh *surely* you know Mrs Northcote-McPherson," said Katie. "She's almost the only person in the village who doesn't want to go ahead with the seal cull."

"She owns half the land in the district," said Tom, "though she hasn't lived here long. They say she was a famous scientist—and from the things she says, she seems to know all about seals."

"I see, I see," mused the Captain; but for some moments he had been watching the horizon like a hawk and, following his eyes, they saw that the line separating sea and sky seemed to be disappearing into an opaque, fuzzy whiteness.

"The mist is coming down," he said, very low, almost more to himself than to them. "We must be turning."

With one quick, deft pull, he started up the engine, turned the boat full circle and soon had it speeding back in the direction of his own island.

"She wants you to come and see her," shouted Tom above the roar of the motor, "urgently. To discuss what we can do."

But the Captain only shook his head at them. "No, no," he said shortly, "there can be no question of that."

"*Please*," said Katie. "She's waiting to see you! It's for the selchies. Look, here's her letter."

"Take the tiller then, laddie," said the Captain, pushing Tom rather roughly into the stern with one hand and taking the envelope from Katie with the other. He tore it open with his teeth and held the flapping paper up to the light. His face was quite expressionless as he read it; and all the while he kept glancing over his shoulder at the rolling mist that drifted steadily on their heels across the waves.

At last he said, "The woman has a fine hand and a pretty turn of phrase. But I cannot accept her invitation."

"But it's for the selchies!" repeated Katie, quite exasperated by the Captain's stubbornness. "You *must* . . ."

"There will be no 'musts' with *me*, lassie!" cried the Captain furiously. "Here, step back lad, let me steer her into land."

They turned into the creek and in the quietness of the chasm his voice sounded loud and commanding. "It is full eleven years since last I did set foot upon the mainland. I told ye before, I have grown bitter and weary with the ways and company of men. I vowed when first I came to work this beacon among the storms that I would never leave; and in all that time I have seen nobody but my two assistants and my only friends, the silver children of the sea whom ye have seen today . . ."

All at once his voice faltered away and for the second time that afternoon his face drained of colour.

As they watched him, puzzled, an inexplicable fear began to creep over Tom and Katie, making them cold and goose-fleshed, and a great heaviness seemed to numb their limbs.

"Oh, oh," said the Captain at last, very faintly, "it is coming again. It comes in the wake of the mist." He·sat down heavily on the stone staircase and hung his head wearily between his knees. "Listen," he whispered. "Och, I had hoped . . . but . . . no, only listen."

At first they heard nothing. Then they caught wind of a distant rumbling, hollow and far-off, with the unearthly quality of thunder. Slowly it grew, smoothly, coming ever closer, until it melted at last into a long, low, vibrating whistle.

"Is it a fog-horn?" whispered Tom. He was surprised to find that his own voice shook. He glanced at Katie: she touched him in reassurance and her hand was icy and damp with fear.

"There is no fog-horn I have ever heard like that," murmured the Captain. "This is the very same sound that I have often heard at night. It comes only when sight is dimmed; and in its wake I have often spied through my glass the shadow of a huge vessel that sails shrouded in blackness."

Even as he spoke, the sound grew louder: a smooth, musical booming, deep and mournful. It seemed to be calling, calling...like an urgent mystical summons.

They each felt rooted there, with neither the courage nor the will-power to move.

But then the sound began to fade, like an ebbing tide, as if it were being swallowed up into the waves from whence it came.

"I thought when first I heard it," said the Captain, speaking now like one waking from a trance, "that it was some new music of the selchies. But it is not, for I have seen them shuddering, just as you do, when it has been upon them." He gave a wry laugh. "Ye may think I am a fanciful man. But I tell ye—something evil is at the bottom of this."

Soon there was silence again except for the lapping water and the distant sound of breakers; overhead, the thick, white curtain of mist was lifting steadily from the sky.

"Now my friends," said the Captain in a gentler tone, "I believe the mist will not settle; but nevertheless, ye must hurry back before dusk. Your thoughts have been chilled enough for one day."

"But what about Mrs Northcote-McPherson?"

said Tom. "What are we going to tell her?"

"Ye will tell her this," declared the Captain, looking anxiously at his watch and standing up. "Ye will tell her that my beacon will not cease its vigilance. Day and night I will be watching. Aye, and ye will tell her that I cannot come to land but that she—for the sake of the selchies—is welcome to visit me."

"But she'll never come, don't you see...she *couldn't*," exclaimed Katie. "She's much too old and lumpy . . . Oh, whatever are we going to do?" For the Captain was already half-way up the steps. "And what about the selchies..."

"Aye, what about them, what about them, lassie?" repeated the Captain, turning to look her full in the eye for a moment—almost mockingly she thought. And then he was disappearing up the last few steps and they heard the echo of his tread across the rocky plateau as he went hurrying off to his lonely beacon.

7   Bitter Words

The children did not meet again until the following Saturday; and then, when she saw Tom, Katie knew at once that something was wrong.

For he came up to their favourite meeting place at the end of the old wooden pier with a scowl on his face, half-heartedly kicking a stone before him and not even bothering to put up his hood against the raw drizzle.

"I wrote a letter to Mrs Northcote-McPherson like we agreed," said Katie after they'd exchanged 'hellos', "telling her everything that the Captain said. I dropped it through her letter-box and I'm sure I heard her coming out to see what it was; but I didn't dare face her on my own, so I ran off as quickly as I could. I haven't heard anything from her though—have you?"

"Nope."

"What's up Tom?" she asked sharply. "Is it about the selchies?"

He shrugged and kicked his stone hard into the harbour where it fell with a satisfying splash.

"Kate—I've got something to tell you."

He said it in such a wretched way that her heart gave a little jump.

"Go on then."

"Well," he said, and she could tell he was trying to disguise the huskiness in his voice, "we're moving. Leaving the village. Next month."

"*What?*"

"My dad's got a job," said Tom, rushing now to get it out, "a really good one. In Glasgow. He says the fishing's never ever going to pick up again and he reckons this is an opportunity . . ."

". . . In *Glasgow?*"

". . . A wonderful opportunity for us all. We've got to adapt, he says, and there'll be better . . ."

"But Tom," she cried, unable to bear it any longer, "Glasgow's over 200 miles away! It's a different world! I'll never see you again—you'll be stuck out there in a dirty old city full of millions of people! You'll soon forget all about the mountains and the sea . . ."

"I know, I know, I know," he said.

". . . And the deer in the woods, and watching the geese fly over in the spring. And what about all the islands we were going to explore together? We've hardly even started—oh, Tom! All you'll ever see there are houses and cars and factories . . ."

"Stop it!" he shouted. He had been doing his very best not to think of precisely all these things and now, as she listed them the lump in his throat grew bigger and bigger until he had to turn away and blink hard.

"But my dad says it's the only sensible thing to do," he said hoarsely. "He'll not listen to anything against the idea; once he's made up his mind, that's it."

"Well, whatever he says, you should refuse to go with him," declared Katie. "*I* wouldn't go. My mum and dad have been talking about that sort of thing too, but I've told them already, if they do, they'll have to leave me behind!"

"Don't be stupid!" said Tom. "How could I possibly stay here? I've got no choice. Where would I live? We're giving up our house and everything."

"Then, then..." she turned away and looked wildly about her, desperately searching for something in the wet afternoon on which to focus her anger. "Then—perhaps we shouldn't try to stop them killing the selchies after all. I mean, it's their fault really, isn't it? It *must* be, yes of course it is! Everyone says so. Where else can all the fish have disappeared to?"

Tom stared at her in shocked disbelief, while the drizzle made small, thudding dents in the harbour water. At first he thought maybe it was a particularly mean way of teasing him, but her face was set and she would not meet his eye.

At last he said: "But Katie, you heard the Captain say that the seals are going hungry too. So how can it be them that's taking the fish?"

Katie took a deep breath and swallowed hard, as if it were her pride she were swallowing. "I'm beginning to think we've been taken in," she said.

She sat down on the edge of the pier and started to tear up a dead leaf that had blown there.

"You see, I've been thinking about it all. I wasn't going to say anything at first because I wasn't sure and it was all so exciting, finding the message in a bottle, landing on the lighthouse island, and sharing a secret with the Captain. But be honest, Tom, when you think about the fairy stories he told us — fancy a grown man believing in that! So how do you know all the rest of it — about the selchies being innocent and in danger — isn't make-believe too?"

"But Katie, what about those dreadful noises? You were there, you heard them."

"Fog-horns," she said curtly.

"You didn't think that when you heard them! I saw you — trembling all over — you were scared out of your mind!"

"It's the Captain suggesting things, and playing on our imaginations," said Katie. "He's got that funny way about him — as if he's hypnotising you — so that you end up believing in all his fantasies."

"All right then," said Tom, "what about Mrs Northcote-McPherson? Surely you don't think that *she's* completely mad too?"

"Well I've never met anyone quite like her before, so I don't know *what* to think," declared Katie pompously, watching a huge, plump figure, wrapped from head to toe in bright yellow oilskins, waddle urgently as fast it could along the harbour wall. "Sometimes I think the whole village is full of funny people — I mean look!"

The newcomer climbed clumsily down into a boat next to the *Clansman*, gave a hefty tug on the motor and began to chug out of the harbour, huddled down in the vessel, looking just like a misshapen and over-inflated balloon.

"Well talking of funny people," said Tom, "I've never seen anyone quite so slimy as Edward da Silva before. So what do you think about *him* Katie, because *he's* the one who's invented the seal-cull?"

"Edward da Silva?" said Katie, kicking her heels against the timbers of the pier, "oh he's . . . he's just a typical city person, that's all. I expect Glasgow will be full of people like that—you wait and see. But at least he's come up with a solution."

"Huh," said Tom, "I'd do almost anything to make the fish come back, you know I would, but I don't believe Mr da Silva's nasty scheme . . ."

"*You* wouldn't kill the selchies whoever suggested it!" cried Katie. "You couldn't—you're too soft and sentimental—just like the barmy old Captain . . ."

"But I thought we agreed about it," cried Tom, getting more and more agitated. "You were as suspicious of Mr da Silva as I was at the beginning. After all, why should someone like him bother coming all the way up here to help us unless he's got some other reason, something that *he's* going to get out of it?"

"Well I dare say he'll get paid for what he's doing," she said reasonably. "That's what usually happens isn't it? I agree, I *did* feel sorry for the selchies at first, perhaps I even still do; yes, I know when we saw them in the water the other day how sweet and almost human they looked..."

"You haven't seen the pups at really close quarters yet," said Tom, crouching down to her level and putting on the most persuasive voice he could muster. "But I saw some once, from just a few inches away, a few years ago. They're all small and white and fluffy, Kate, completely helpless, and their eyes are so big and black that..."

"Yes yes, I *know*," said Katie. "Oh please don't make me feel sorry for them, Tom, what good will it do? Look, everything's different now that you're going," she went on fiercely. "I wouldn't care a crab's claw about killing the sweetest little seal pup in the world if it would only bring the fish back and save you from having to go to Glasgow."

"You talk a load of old rubbish," said Tom, "but worst of all, Kate, you can't ever make up your mind."

"That's nonsense! I bet I've thought about it far more than you have! You're not even pleased I want to save you!"

"Why should I be pleased, when you're so heartless about hurting innocent animals? I just don't see why you should suddenly turn about like this..."

"Oh shut up!" she shouted, leaping up and stamping her foot at him. "I'm fed up with my dad having no work and no money and the whole village going to seed, that's why! There's nothing heartless about that!"

They stood there in the drizzle, glaring at each other. It was as if somebody had taken their friendship and, before their eyes, snipped it into tiny, useless pieces.

At length Tom said, "All right then, go and help shoot them if that's what you want. I hope it does you good. And listen: I'm *glad* I'm leaving. Yes I am! Glad to get away from you—and from all the other thick stupid people in the village who won't see any further than their own noses. I'm still sure the Captain and Mrs Northcote-McPherson are right, but I don't even care any more, because *I'm* going."

He turned abruptly on his heel and began to walk rapidly away from her, up to the main street and towards his house.

8   Incriminating Evidence

Tom had only walked a short way before he decided that he did not want to go home after all. There would be nothing there to cheer him: only his mother packing clothes and sorting linen and his father clearing out the attic and measuring furniture; and everywhere cluttered up with boxes and packing cases.

So instead of following the road to his cottage on the lower slopes of the hill, he turned off onto a narrow footpath leading to the low, rocky cliffs around the bay.

He decided to go for a long walk. It would be the first of many: a farewell series of walks. Only last summer he had made a secret list of all his favourite, hidden places on the hills and along the coast; and now, as he marched along, he planned to visit each one of them in turn; and perhaps he would even discover some new ones. At any rate, he would go alone.

It was just typical of Katie to turn about like that, he thought angrily. She was always so petulant, so quick to lose her temper and her sense. If only they could have stopped the cull together before he had to leave—somehow then he wouldn't have minded going so much. It would at least have been a comfort to know that the seals were still around, even if in the end all the people had to go....

The path led upwards over steep, slippery gravel and he pressed on with strong, angry strides. The rain had stopped and he threw back the hood of his anorak with relief. Immediately a biting wind, straight off the sea, whipped around his ears. It tore at his clothing and tried to tumble him over, but he only laughed and whistled fiercely back at it.

Up on the cliff top he stopped for a moment to watch the view. The wide, restless ocean went on for ever, and amongst the waves, scores of tiny islands showed up as craggy black dots; and there was the stark, white beacon of the lighthouse rock. For the first time he thought he understood the Captain's need of solitude.

Then he was off again, running with the wind and the pale, gliding gulls that any day now would be turning to head inland for the winter. He wondered sadly whether any of them would be wintering in Glasgow.

At length he found he was heading downhill again and soon he arrived in a sheltered cove where many large, sea-smoothed boulders lay all over the white beach. He was a little out of breath and hungry, so he sat down on one of the stones and felt about in the pocket of his anorak for something to eat. He pulled out half a packet of fudge wrapped in sticky paper and stuffed it ravenously into his mouth.

Suddenly, he thought he heard a sound.

A small sound, vague as a breath of wind: a catch in the air, like somebody sobbing.

He looked around, but of course he was alone. It's only the waves, he thought, and began to suck on the last piece of the sweet.

But then he jumped and almost choked. There it was again!

His heart missed a beat. I'm imagining things, he thought. And then he saw a rock *move*. Yes, it really was moving!...but it was not a rock at all—it was a seal! A selchie!

He heard the noise again. It really did sound as if somebody was crying. It must be the selchie.

He sat dead still, not daring to move. What would it do if it saw him? But then he realised that the selchie had seen him already. It was staring straight at him, almost as if it were waiting.

Slowly, slowly, he got up from the rock. The creature watched him from large, unblinking eyes. Then it let out another sob.

He crept towards it on tiptoe at first, because he did not want it to shy away. But as he drew nearer, he began to understand why the selchie showed no fear. Its stare was one not of trust, but of sorrowful indifference. It was numbed and senseless with grief.

Because stretched out on the sand beside it was the heavy, lifeless body of another seal.

Tom gasped and turned away. He was not afraid simply because it was dead—he had seen plenty of dead sheep and rabbits on the hills and beaches. But there was something peculiar about it, and something disturbing about the way in which the live selchie was guarding the corpse. Unnatural. Almost as if . . . as if it had been murdered.

Don't be daft, he thought to himself, animals can't be murdered. Animals were slaughtered, for meat or hides, or because they were pests. Only people could be murdered.

And yet—it was true what the Captain had said, there *was* something uncannily human about them. For the live selchie had its gaze riveted upon him; and now that he was barely a few feet away, he could see right into its large, moist eyes: they were as deep and as sad as the oceans. As he watched, it let two tears fall, one from one eye, and one from the other.

Tom bit his lip and bent towards the seal. "Hello," he said softly, "what's wrong?"

The seal glanced for a moment at the body beside it and then turned its sorrowful gaze back to him. But it did not sob again.

"Who killed your friend?" asked Tom, crouching down and pointing. It seemed quite natural that they should hold a sort of conversation, Tom in a respectful whisper, and the selchie answering him through the changing depths and shades of its eyes.

Although he did not really want to, Tom decided that he ought to take a closer look at the body. So he trod a slow, wide circle around it; and when he was half-way between the seal's head and the sea, he stopped suddenly.

In front of the dead creature's open jaws and eagerly grasping flippers was an untidy pile of fish.

There were three large cod, two mackerel and the head and belly of a huge, silver salmon. The wind had almost dried them out now and they were beginning to stench because they had not been gutted. Yet clearly they had once held all the promise of a luscious feast. Indeed, it looked as if it was excess greed that had been the main cause of the creature's death.

But where did the fish come from, when not a single one, dead or alive, had been seen in the village for weeks?

He was puzzling over this astonishing discovery when his eyes fell on two small objects lying on the sand, and his heart leapt because he knew at once that these must be vital clues.

One was the cardboard carton from a roll of photographic film. The other was an empty brass cartridge-case from a gun.

In a flash, despondency and weariness disappeared: to be replaced by anger. The Captain was right, he thought: I knew it, I *knew* it!

He could hear the waves breaking and trickling back over the shingle: his thoughts caught the rhythm and worked with it slowly, surely, until a meaning began to emerge.

The bullet: well, the wound must be concealed under the dead seal's body.

But the film? And the fish?

Of course, he thought, this tableau would make a

striking photograph of a seal caught red-handed in the act of swallowing the last remnants of the coastline's disappearing fish. And anyone who looked at the size of its blubber-swollen body would expect it to take rather more than five and a half fish to keep *that* going for very long! Which must have been exactly the impression that the photographer meant to convey when he killed the seal and posed it before his camera.

"Well," said Tom out loud, "well, well, well." And the live selchie looked at him expectantly.

But who was the photographer and what was he going to do with his photograph? A name and a face flashed irresistibly into Tom's mind. Hastily he began to memorise everything that he had found. There was so little time: he must go to Mrs Northcote-McPherson and she, of course, would need to know every detail if she were to act upon it.

He was fairly certain that he would be able to mark this spot on the map; but just to make sure that he could find it again he would calculate its position by counting exactly how many paces it took him to walk back.

He looked again as hard as he could at the whole scene, counting the rocks and trying to guess heights and distances. He even searched in case there were footprints which might incriminate someone by the mark of a particular pair of boots; but it was so windy down there that even his own fresh tracks had already been covered by a new layer of sand.

Next he turned his attention to the dead seal,

noting exactly how it had been laid out and the marks in the sand beside it. Then he picked up the bullet and the carton from the film and put them in the secret zipper-pocket in the lining of his anorak: these were the only concrete clues that he could take back and he would risk anything rather than lose them.

Finally, he took one last look at the heap of fish and said out loud: "Three cod, two mackerel and half a salmon," and, as if in reply, the selchie that was keeping vigil let out another of its throaty, haunting sobs.

Tom went up to it as close as he dared and crouched down to its level.

"Hey," he said, "listen. I'm on your side. I'm going to help you." He felt like a wartime conspirator, making a pact with a foreign but trusted ally. "I'm going to stop the people who want to kill you all—whatever happens, I don't care—somehow—I will!" He paused. "Do you understand?" he whispered.

The selchie made neither move nor sound. But he thought he saw something changing in its eyes— almost imperceptibly—as if a cloud were lifting.

He stood up. "I've got to go. It's a long way back. But I swear I'll do everything I can."

There was not a sound apart from the waves beating ceaselessly upon the beach.

"We'll probably never meet again," he said "so—goodbye."

He hesitated for a moment before turning to

retrace his steps back to the cliff-top path. Already he was counting his paces diligently. But when he got to twenty, something made him stop and look back; and as he did so, he saw the selchie shifting as if it were about to leave its sentry-post at last.

He stared at it and—for an instant and even across that distance, their eyes met.

There was something in that gaze—an understanding. And although Katie laughed at the idea when he told her about it afterwards, he knew that it contained a sort of promise. He was sure that the selchie was telling him, "I will do what I can for you as well."

But it was only a brief flash of sympathy, because the next moment the selchie had turned away from him and was lumbering into the sea.

9   Vagabond!

After Tom had stormed off, Katie stood gazing out to sea for some time. Her head throbbed and she felt listless. Everything seemed to be in a muddle, everything seemed to be going wrong. She ran into the village for an ice-cream from McCodrum's store and then back to the harbour to eat it. But it was too cold for ice-cream: it made her teeth tingle and sent a shiver through her from head to foot.

How eerily quiet everything was: the quayside should have been full of fishing-boats unloading, with the men shouting and singing and the women stopping for a gossip on the way to the shop. But today—like every day now—there was nobody here at all.

As she lingered there she caught the sound of a distant engine and then a small boat, navigated by a familiar-looking, rotund, yellow figure, came into view and chugged into the harbour.

It had scarcely reached its mooring before a voice was yelling: "Katherine!" with such suddenness that Katie almost jumped right out of her skin.

"It is Katherine, isn't it? Quick girl, give me a hand up for goodness' sake, I can't wait about here for ever!"

"Mrs Northcote-McPherson!" cried Katie, when at last the large, panting lady was standing beside her on the quayside. "I had no idea it was you!"

"Well you jolly well ought to have done," declared Mrs Northcote-McPherson crossly, removing her large-brimmed sou'wester and shaking her iron-grey curls free. "Why, I only passed you a short while ago: you want to keep your eyes open, young lady! Now, since by the looks of things you've got nothing useful to do, perhaps you can help me. I want to hear everything you know about the Captain."

"Oh!" said Katie, trying to think quickly, but forgetting everything in her confusion. "The Captain?...I...We told you everything when we came to see you."

"I've just come back from his island," said Mrs Northcote-McPherson shortly. "Humph! He nearly fell of his rock with surprise, poor fellow. Said he wasn't expecting to see me. Said he'd heard I was too delicate to take to sea!" She snorted and looked accusingly at Katie. "What! Didn't I spend the best part of my life sailing through the tropical storms of the South Pacific in a dug-out canoe, with only my dear, departed Algernon for company? You'll not find a couple of waves defeating Hermione Northcote-McPherson, *that's* for sure!"

Katie blushed uncomfortably; but Mrs Northcote-McPherson only stamped hard to warm herself and then continued in a kinder tone:

"He's a funny old chap though, don't you think so, my dear?"

"I'm sure he's completely mad," declared Katie boldly; after all, Mrs Northcote-McPherson always seemed to speak her mind, so why shouldn't she? "All those soppy fairy tales he goes on about!"

"The selchie legends? Don't believe in them myself, but there's no smoke without fire, don't you know?" She replaced her sou'wester and assumed a businesslike air. "But listen," she went on, "there's reason enough for us to doubt his sanity, eh? And yet something—dear Algernon would have called it feminine intuition—tells me that there's more to the man than meets the eye. However, the only facts are that he hears noises—strange, inexplicable noises. And at irregular intervals he sees an apparition..."

Katie stared at her and swallowed. Suddenly, her own shivering encounter with the whistling summons from the deep loomed up again in her mind's eye, so vividly that her heart started to pound, just as it had on that misty afternoon last week.

"...By all accounts, one ought to call him mad," continued Mrs Northcote-McPherson. "A man who shuns the company of others is bound in the end to start imagining things and..."

"But I heard it too!" Katie burst out, "the noise I mean. So did Tom. It was...oh, so weird!"

"Gracious, child," exclaimed Mrs Northcote-McPherson, standing back to look at her, as if to assure herself that Katie was not making it up. "You did, did you? All three of you heard it at once?

Humph! It's most unlikely that you would *all* have been imagining the same thing. It seems that my hunch is right and we must get a move on! There's no time to lose! Now then, I need someone to help me while I make some observations—can you spare an hour or so?"

Before Katie could even reply, Mrs Northcote-McPherson had climbed down into the boat again, started up the engine and was beckoning to her to follow.

"You can read a compass, can't you?" she called as she took the boat out onto the open sea.

Katie nodded.

"Then direct me as I steer!" commanded Mrs Northcote-McPherson, opening up the throttle of the engine as far as it would go. With a roar, the boat leapt into the full force of the wind, riding the swell as graciously as a duck. Katie crouched low, to avoid the chilly waves which kept washing over them; but Mrs Northcote-McPherson stood firm at the helm, one hand on the tiller, her grey curls streaming in the wind, her handsome face smiling, looking for all the world like some proud warrior queen.

"We're hunting for the ship," she yelled over the motor. "This dark apparition. The Captain's vision. It appears to have a direct link with the noises. He reckoned he'd caught sight of it on the skyline less than twenty minutes before I arrived at his island; but he said it turned back almost at once before he could be sure, as if it were trying to hide itself.

Which way are we heading?"

"North-north-west," Katie shouted back, pushing her salty-damp hair out of her eyes.

Mrs Northcote-McPherson turned the rudder abruptly and the boat swung round.

"And now?"

"Almost due west," said Katie.

"Splendid, splendid! He says he always sees it in the far west. But I'll tell you something else ... are my binoculars there?"

"Where?"

"Under the seat, girl—for goodness' sake use your eyes! Yes? Good. Now as I was saying—we had a good chat together, this Captain fellow and I. Knows an awful lot about seals. Studied them day and night. Why, he knows almost as much about them as I do about the Galapagos iguana!"

"I know," said Katie. "He took us out to see them. He knew exactly where to find them."

"I should certainly think he did! And that's why I pay attention to what he says. He's got a most interesting hypothesis."

"Pardon?" said Katie.

"Humph. A theory. A plausible idea. You know, nobody's ever actually proved exactly what these grey seals do eat: they spend most of their time too far out at sea to study their habits properly. But the Captain holds that they don't eat fish; well, not very much anyway."

"Oh, but they *must* do," insisted Katie, "if they live in the sea. That's where all *our* fish are going ..."

"Eels," said Mrs Northcote-McPherson firmly.

"Pardon?" said Katie again.

"He reckons they eat eels. Conger eels. Nasty long things, with big jaws full of teeth. And eels eat fish, of course, so if the seals eat the eels, they're doing *us* a service, after all, by leaving more fish ... wait! What's that?"

She stood rigidly to attention and pointed straight ahead. At first Katie could see nothing, but gradually she made out a spot in the far distance where one oblong patch of cloud, hanging low over the horizon, seemed unnaturally darker than the rest.

"Can you steer?" asked Mrs Northcote-McPherson, talking fast but precisely. "Pass me the binoculars and grab hold of the tiller!"

While Katie steered with a tight, nervous grip, Mrs Northcote-McPherson pulled the glasses out of their black leather case with feverish hands.

"Yes!" she exclaimed, "I was right! Look, Katherine, look through the glasses!"

She pressed the binoculars to Katie's eyes.

Sure enough, so far away that it was almost below the horizon's curve, lay the mass of a huge, grey, windowless ship.

"Now," said Mrs Northcote-McPherson, allowing a slight tremor of excitement into her voice, "slow down. We must get a little closer—but not close enough for them to hear us. With any luck we're probably too small and far away to have been spotted yet. We may have to turn off the engine soon and drift with the current. All I want is one thing and I shall be satisfied—and that's to get the name of the ship."

"What about the noises?" asked Katie as they drifted closer. "I can't hear them yet."

But before Mrs Northcote-McPherson could answer, another, quite unexpected sound assailed their ears. It was the whine of a speed boat.

Mrs Northcote-McPherson glanced up and then adjusted the binoculars feverishly. At last she had them right and, while she stared fixedly through them at the mysterious ship, with her free hand she began to feel in the pocket of her voluminous oilskins.

"I can see it!" she exclaimed. "I can just make out the name. Ha! Here's pencil and paper—take it, Katherine, will you? Let's go in a little closer. That's right. Now—you'd better stop the engine. And listen carefully because I want you to write this down."

Katie waited, pencil poised. The little dinghy bobbed up and down, frail as a bird on the grey expanse of ocean. And all the while, the searing whine of the speed-boat grew steadily nearer.

"V . . . A . . . G . . ." Mrs Northcote-McPherson spelt out, ". . . A . . . B . . . O . . . N . . ."

Zzzzooom! The speed-boat swept into view in a curtain of spray and it seemed that any moment now it would be upon them!

"Vagabond!" cried Mrs Northcote-McPherson, and it was half a statement, half an accusation flung into the wind at this new and unwelcomed arrival. "Write it down! And note this too—it's registered in Amsterdam. Now—quick—it's coming for us— start the engine up and let's get back!"

"Oh I can't!" cried Katie, pulling desperately, again and again, on the starter. She felt simultaneously hot and cold with panic. "It won't go!"

The speed-boat was circling them, menacing, threatening, in gradually diminishing circles.

"What's the matter, you foolish girl?" cried Mrs Northcote-McPherson furiously, flinging down the binoculars and seizing Katie roughly by the shoulder. "I thought you said you could handle a boat!"

Zzzzooom! screamed the other boat's engine: closer and closer it came.

"I am *not* foolish!" retorted Katie, turning red with rage, "I'm *not*! There's no petrol in it—that's what's wrong!"

"Goodness gracious!" cried Mrs Northcote-McPherson. "Petrol! There should be a spare can under the seat—that's right."

The other boat was so near that its spray was actually splashing them and they could clearly see its pilot—a tall, straight man wearing a black wet-suit, his face almost hidden by a huge pair of goggles.

In their urgency neither of them noticed something else in the water: a dark, liquid shadow, barely below the surface, breaking the diminishing distance between their boat and the intruder.

Somehow, although their hands were icy cold

and wet and clouds of water veiled their sight, they managed to unscrew the cap of the petrol can and to pour the greenish liquid into the engine. Mrs Northcote-McPherson pulled hard on the starter and this time it roared into life.

"Move over child—out of the way!" she yelled fiercely, yanking the tiller so that the boat turned right round. At that moment, Katie saw the underwater shadow and screamed; the speed-boat veered out of their path; and suddenly, seven glistening bull-seals rose up out of the water half-way between their own boat and their pursuers with a blood-curdling roar!

In and out they dived, a solid, living wall, easily strong enough to tumble a mere speed-launch into the sea. The pilot lurched this way and that, seeking a clear path through the waves; but always the seals blocked his way.

Katie stared and blinked, numb and helpless with amazement. But Mrs Northcote-McPherson was as staunch as a lioness; she batted not an eyelid as she guided the boat back to land.

When at last their pursuer was no more than a wildly zigzagging dot in the distance and the seals had disappeared, she stood up again, waving her fist at the sky.

"I know how to deal with vagabonds!" she shouted. "Remember the name, Katherine! Aha, *I* won't forget it in a hurry!"

"But what was he trying to do?" asked Katie. Now that they were out of danger again she found herself trembling all over and even the robust Mrs Northcote-McPherson looked rather pale.

The lady only shook her head and sat down stiffly on the bench in front of the tiller.

"It's obvious enough what he was trying to do," she muttered, "but *why* . . . ?" She shook her head again and they sailed back to the little harbour without another word.

But all the while, a number of new and disturbing questions went spinning round and round in Katie's head. Where did the seals come from, so miraculously just in time? And why did they want to save her and Mrs Northcote-McPherson? Did they, as the Captain said, have some magic "second sight", some way of sensing an enemy—and an ally?

And then a hot wave of guilt flooded through her. Here she was, accusing the selchies—ready to kill them; and yet the selchies had saved her unhesitatingly, as if she had been an innocent friend.

She felt wretched . . . but then the familiar sight of the wooden jetty and the sad, empty boats appeared again, and her head cleared until there was but one unshakeable idea left. The seals have given me a chance, she thought, and I'll show them—I've got to show them—they were right.

"You're a sensible sort of girl after all," said Mrs Northcote-McPherson kindly when they were on dry land once more. She unpeeled herself noisily from her oilskins, breathing a sigh of relief. "You've been a big help. We'll be in touch again."

"But what about the ship," asked Katie, "and the seals?"

But Mrs Northcote-McPherson was already half-way along the pier. "There'll be time for explanations when everything's said and done," she called, "but right now there's too much to do. I'm sorry my dear, but I haven't a minute to spare—I've very urgent enquiries to make and I simply *must* put a 'phone call through to London!"

Bad Luck

Somebody had been very busy during the night.
For, next morning, wherever you looked around
the straggling, whitewashed village, you could see
giant red posters on walls, windows and trees.

Tom was so absorbed in examining one outside
the village hall, that he did not hear footsteps
running up behind him; and he jumped when
Katie's voice suddenly said:

"'Lo Tom."

"Oh! Hello."

There was an awkward silence while they
avoided each others' eyes.

"Well," said Katie quickly, "I must hurry, my
mum wants me to get some things at McCodrum's
and they close early today. But I..." She seemed
about to say more; then, changing her mind she
turned instead to cross the road.

"Kate!" said Tom urgently. "Have you seen
these?" He pointed at the poster.

She looked round, shaking her head. "Not
properly, I've been in such a rush...oh!" She
started back, wide-eyed.

A SEAL'S LIFE OR YOUR LIVELIHOOD!
EVERY SEAL KILLED HELPS TO BRING
OUR FISH BACK TO THE SEAS! COME
TO THE CULL ON SATURDAY

It was the photograph underneath that took her breath away; its crude, simple message was clearly designed to shock. It showed a huge seal sprawled on a beach, its jaws open in the act of eating; and in front of it, a large pile of glimmering, wet fish.

"Kate," whispered Tom, "that photograph..."

But Katie had paled and was staring at it with a look of bewilderment on her face.

"Is it true?" she murmured. She had no doubt now what she *wanted* to believe, but what good was that unless she could be sure? "Tom," her voice shook a little, "do you think...? Tell me honestly... *have* they stolen all our fish?"

"No!" cried Tom, grabbing her arm and shaking it roughly in his agitation. "I'm not just guessing this time—I'm certain! Don't you see? It's a fake. *I've seen how they did it!*"

"Whatever do you mean?" she asked sharply.

"I wish you weren't so stubborn!" cried Tom. "I wish we could still be friends and stop the cull together! It's *their* fish as much as ours that's gone, Kate; and I've got evidence that I'm going to see Mrs Northcote-McPherson about, whether or not you want to help."

"Before you go Tom...I've got something to tell you."

"Well?"

"Something's happened to me. I feel differently about the selchies now, I'll even admit I was wrong. Because...they saved my life."

He blinked at her as if she were going as crazy as the Captain.

"And Mrs Northcote-McPherson too," she went on. "She got me involved in it all you see, after you stormed off. We sailed out to find the Captain's mysterious dark ship—we've actually seen it—and then this speed-boat came and tried to sink us, and if it wasn't for the selchies, we'd both have been killed."

"Well somebody killed the selchie that I saw," said Tom, determined not to be too impressed, "to take this photograph. And whoever it was got hold of the fish from somewhere. And more than that— I've got some clues that might even prove who it was. If you're *really* sorry Kate, I might let you come with me to see Mrs Northcote-McPherson, even though you were so rotten."

"I wasn't rotten," said Katie crossly, "it was you. And I don't see what's so special about going to see Mrs Northcote-McPherson, especially after I've had a whole adventure with her, all by myself. But if you want me to come with you, you'll have to wait while I go to McCodrum's."

So Tom followed her across the road, through the glass door with the loudly jangling bell and into the small, tightly-packed store.

Behind the cluttered counter Mrs McCodrum

waited, wiping her freckled hands on a neat, floral-printed apron.

"Good afternoon Katie," she said, "and Tom isn't it? What can I do for you?"

"My mum says, have you a loaf of bread left?" said Katie. "And half a dozen eggs."

"Now I can help you with the bread, Katie," said Mrs McCodrum, reaching up to one of the shelves behind her for a brown, crusty loaf, "but as for the eggs I've clean sold out. Och, and there's a story behind that, if you've the time to hear it."

"Oh yes," said Katie, "go on."

"Well," said Mrs McCodrum, folding her arms and settling down for a good gossip. "You'll have heard of this Mr da Silva who's come up from London to kill the selchies?"

Tom had been browsing restlessly around with one eye on his watch, anxious to be off to Mrs Northcote-McPherson's; but at these words he looked up and came to lean against the counter beside Katie to hear Mrs McCodrum's tale.

"Now," continued Mrs McCodrum, "he was staying at *Alt-na-Tigh*, old Mrs Hamish's guest-house. And very pleased she was too, to have a guest at this time of year. But listen, would you believe it—the very night he moved in, she was taken ill! Her, Widow Hamish, who's always been as strong and healthy as a horse! She had to be rushed off to hospital, poor thing—out of the blue it was, a very serious illness. So Mr da Silva had to leave."

"Where did he go?" asked Tom.

"Well you know, everyone else closes down for the winter, so at first it looked like there'd be nowhere for him. But folks wouldn't have that, after he came all the way up here to help us, so in the end Angus and Morag Dougall took him in, and put him up in their spare room."

"But what's that got to do with the eggs?" asked Katie.

"Now half a mo'," scolded Mrs McCodrum, who hated nothing more than to be rushed when she was telling a story. "I'll be coming to that. Now, what do you think happened only the next morning after he went there?"

"What?" asked Tom, starting to feel impatient with her prattle.

"Well, if old Angus didn't get a phone call from his son Alex—you remember him now—saying he was in hospital in Inverness, having been knocked off his motor-bike and broken both his legs."

"How awful!" said Katie.

"Yes, so the Dougalls wasted no time in going down to see the lad; and Mr da Silva, being a polite gentleman, left as soon as he could and now he's hiring a caravan on the site above the village. Looking after himself, he is, so that's why he came to buy some eggs. Half a dozen extra large I sold him—and then if he wasn't back within half an hour complaining that every single one was rotten and asking for some more!

"'I'll try one before I take them with me,' he says, so I gave him a cup to crack it in, and blow me, if that wasn't rotten too! And then he tried every one of my last remaining dozen, and each was the same. So I bundled him out quick and down I sat here and had a good, long think."

"It's a bit strange, isn't it?" said Katie.

"Aye, it is that. Those eggs were all as fresh as daisies, delivered only yesterday from Brodie's Farm; and we've been buying them in from there for full fifteen years with never yet a cause for complaint."

"Mr da Silva must attract bad luck," said Tom thoughtfully.

"Well, I can't say that I'm surprised," said Mrs McCodrum. She leaned forward to them across the counter and lowered her voice.

"'Tis the magic of the selchies," she whispered.

Tom's heart jumped: it was as if he could see again the weeping selchie on the lonely beach, could sense the understanding which had passed between them. His voice came out unnaturally shrill: "Whatever do you mean?"

"'Twas my mother as would always tell me this, when I was nought but a wee bairn at her knee," said Mrs McCodrum. "'Never do harm by the selchies,' were her words, 'and they'll never do harm by you.' Aye, for 'tis said that they will not in a lifetime forget a turn that is once done to them, be it good or bad . . . But 'tis full forty years since last I heard it said."

"Is it true?" asked Tom. "How can it be? Can they *really* make things happen?"

Mrs McCodrum shrugged and shook her head. "There are many things we can never understand, Tom," she said. "Now, before he went rushing off, Angus Dougall declared it was all coincidence and no more, and he's told everyone that, come what may, his boats will be available for the cull. And yet—well, we all know Mr da Silva has given us the idea of killing the seals; and now everything and everyone he mixes with is going bad. Myself, I am almost afraid to serve him again in case the curse is catching.

"But look at the time! I must be closing now. Here is the loaf of bread for your mother, Katie."

Katie paid for it and they made their way out; but by the door, Tom stopped, for there was a small display of photographic equipment that he had not seen before.

"Oh, Mrs McCodrum," he called, "I didn't realise you sell films. Do you have any of this sort?"

He pulled from his pocket the empty cardboard carton he had found by the dead seal on the beach and held it out to show her.

Mrs McCodrum looked at it and then at Tom with a queer expression in her eyes.

"No," she said slowly, "I don't. Indeed, I have never even seen one before—until this morning, that is, when Mr da Silva came in. Strange to say, Tom, he was asking for exactly the same one. 'Not to worry,' he says, 'I didn't expect you would stock it. I bought this one in Amsterdam,' he says, 'so perhaps you can't buy them over here.'"

"In Amsterdam?" said Tom.

"In Amsterdam!" exclaimed Katie, but under her breath, so that Mrs McCodrum should not hear. She gulped hard. "Come on Tom," she said, "we'd best get on. Goodbye Mrs McCodrum."

"Goodbye Katie, goodbye Tom."

They ran back to the village hall and sat excitedly side by side on the broad, concrete step.

"It's like a jigsaw!" said Tom. "Listen, here are the pieces. Mr da Silva comes on the scene soon after the fish have disappeared. He tells us to kill the selchies and then immediately brings all sorts of bad luck to anyone who helps him. She's right Kate — she must be — it's a magic sign to show us all that he's wrong!"

"Perhaps so," she said; yet she could feel the last doubts melting away like snow. "Anyway, Mr da Silva must have been to Amsterdam if he bought the film there — and that's where this mysterious ship is registered! Mrs Northcote-McPherson saw it written on the side."

"And he used the film to take the picture of the selchie he killed," said Tom, "and he got hold of some fish from somewhere too. So all the bits tie up together and it all keeps coming back to Edward da Silva."

"The trouble is though, there's so much missing," said Katie. "Like what is this dark ship doing, and what are the noises..."

"And whatever's going to happen to the whole village if they just ignore the selchies' warnings?"

murmured Tom. He bit his nail furiously and tried hard to think.

But Katie was already starting up the road as if her own resolution had never been in question. "Mrs Northcote-McPherson's bound to be able to put it together," she called, "but Tom, if we don't hurry, there won't be enough time for her even to *start* to work it out...."

11   Closed Doors

The resounding boom of a brass door knocker; a
breeze stirring the piles of autumn leaves on the
long, sweeping driveway. An expectant silence,
then a door creaking open and footsteps shuffling
down a passage.

"She's in," said Tom.

The front door opened and a short, sparrow-
faced woman wearing rubber-gloves and a nylon
housecoat confronted them curiously.

"Oh!" said Katie in surprise.

"Is Mrs Northcote-McPherson at home please?"
asked Tom.

"No," said the woman, "she's away."

"Away?" said Katie. "Where's she gone, when
will she be back?"

"Who are you," said the woman, peering down
her thin nose at them, "asking all these questions?"

"We're ... friends of hers," said Tom. "We're
here on very urgent business. We've got something
to tell her, about the s ..."

Katie trod hard on his toe. How could they be
sure which side anyone was on? "Do you have any
idea when she might be back?" she asked politely.

"Won't be for days," said the woman, shaking her head wearily and starting to close the door. "Not till Saturday at the earliest. And she's left me that much cleaning out cupboards and polishing of silver to do as would keep me going for twice as long as that! So if you'll excuse me..."

"Just a minute," said Tom, "*please*. You don't know where she's gone, do you?"

"No!"

"...If we could possibly contact her at all..."

"Look," said the woman, "I don't know who you are, or what your business is, but she's gone *abroad*, see? So that's the end of it."

"Abroad?" said Katie. "You don't know where, do you?"

"I don't know," said the housekeeper crossly, "Holland—Amsterdam I think she said it was. That's all I can tell you, so now you know."

"Please would you let her know we called," said Tom, "when she gets back. Thomas and Katherine, tell her."

"I'll tell her all right!" cried the woman; and the door closed with a dull thud behind her.

"Well that's her out," said Katie as they sloshed their way back down the drive. "Perhaps she'll come up with something in Amsterdam, but that's no help to us at the moment." She stopped for a moment to kick her frustration into a dense cloud of brown, papery leaves. "What are we going to do?"

"I've been thinking," said Tom. "We ought to

go and see the Captain again. Don't forget we promised to bring him all the news."

"Yes, and we've hardly told him anything. And yet everything that's happened fits in with what he told us."

"You called it fairy tales at the time," said Tom accusingly.

"All right, all right," said Katie quickly before he could say any more. "Now come on, we'd better hurry, it'll be getting dark in about an hour."

They ran down to the harbour; it seemed emptier than ever. Even the shrieking gulls had gone away now, for there was no food for them. Nothing disturbed the late afternoon except for the soft creaking of ropes, and the sound of wood bumping against wood as the unused boats rode the incoming tide.

The door of Angus Dougall's rickety old hut was shut fast and a hastily scribbled notice was pinned beneath the rusty lock:

> *Harbour Master regrets urgently called away. All messages to McCodrum's Store. Apologies for inconvenience. Business as usual* FOR CULL ON SATURDAY *and hopefully thereafter.*   AD

"Of course," said Tom, "Mrs McCodrum told us—his son had an accident."

"Well," said Katie, "we'll just have to take the boat without asking, that's all. It's not our fault he's not here."

"We could always tell McCodrums..."

"Tom!" said Katie, "there's no time. Come on."

Several small boats with outboard motors were tied up below the pier. They climbed into the nearest and Katie pulled on the starter.

Nothing happened: not even a spark or a hint of a crackle from the engine.

"Let me try," said Tom impatiently; but he had no more success.

"It's no use," said Katie, "I could have told you that straight away. Exactly the same thing happened when I was out with Mrs Northcote-McPherson. There's no petrol in it."

"Come on then," said Tom, "there's another four to try."

But all the boats were the same: each petrol tank had been drained quite dry and there was no sign anywhere of a can or drum from which to fill them up.

"I bet Mr da Silva's taken it all," said Katie, "because he's frightened someone might sabotage his plans; or find out something he wants to keep hidden—like Mrs Northcote-McPherson and I almost did."

"Well then," said Tom slowly, "there's only one thing for it: we'll have to go to the police."

"I'm not reporting *my* story," said Katie. "I dare not. It's secret. It's up to Mrs Northcote-McPherson to tell anyone if she wants to."

Tom leap-frogged over a bollard and started back towards the village.

"I wish we didn't have to, Kate—I'm sure old PC

99

Stuart is all for the cull. But who else could we go to?"

Constable Stuart, whose solitary beat covered not only the village but also many of the surrounding crofts, lived and worked in rather a plain, yellow-brick house right at the end of the main street. A blue lamp burned day and night in his porch.

They pressed the bell apprehensively. Tinny chimes sounded somewhere inside; and then almost immediately, the policeman appeared in his shirtsleeves.

He was a burly man, with a neatly-trimmed black beard which unsuccessfully tried to conceal his double chin. He raised a friendly eyebrow at them.

"Yes?"

"We'd like to report something, please," said Tom.

"Come in, come in."

He sat them down in his pale grey office amongst large metal filing cabinets and boxes of stationery, and wrote their particulars down in a notebook with black, water-proof covers.

"What's it all about then?"

"It's Tom who's got something to tell you," said Katie, "but I'd just like to say this so that you know we're being serious. We've been to see Mrs Northcote-McPherson and we're er . . ."

"We're working with her," said Tom importantly.

"Mrs Northcote, eh?" said the policeman; and he raised the other eyebrow. "Working with her?"

"Yes," said Katie, "to do with the cull."

He blinked at them both. "I see," he said, and scribbled something in his notebook.

"We've come about this photograph of the seal," said Tom, "the one on Mr da Silva's posters. You see, I've found out—I've got proof—that they're fakes."

"Oh," laughed Constable Stuart, "if *that's* your only problem, you've got nothing to worry about at all! That's very common. Standard practice in fact. It's well known that publicity photographs are often stunts. I expect the seal in this particular picture's a dead one—stuffed? Go on, tell me everything, am I right?"

"It's dead all right," said Tom. "I found the cartridge-case from the bullet that killed it."

"Can't be helped," said the constable, shaking his head and pretending to look grave. "There'll be plenty of bullets and plenty of dead seals on Saturday you know."

"But it's a complete fraud!" cried Tom, "it's a frame-up! These fish . . ."

But PC Stuart only laughed even more heartily and dismissed it without troubling to listen any further.

"McCodrums have still got plenty of frozen fish left in their store," he said. "None of the locals will touch them—superstitious I except. I should imagine Mr da Silva was a welcome customer when he bought them for his picture."

Tom took a deep breath and swallowed his

anger. He caught Katie's eye and willed her to do the same. It wouldn't do if they made fools of themselves: it was a serious game they were caught up in and they had to play it like adults. The turn of events on Saturday might depend upon how they handled the rules.

"Hasn't Mrs Northcote-McPherson been to see you about this?" he asked politely.

"Look lad," said Constable Stuart with a friendly slap on the shoulder which only made Tom cringe, "you must have heard what people say about her. A nice lady, very polite, pleasant, well bred... but well. She's—how can I put it—got too much brains. Too educated. Knows too many things: spent too much of her life studying goodness knows what on some island right on the other side of the world. I wouldn't go taking too much notice of her pronouncements, or meddling in business that you don't understand."

In another room a telephone rang.

Tom said, "But the whole thing's a mistake! Don't you see..."

The door opened and Mrs Stuart poked her head round.

"The lorry's on its way, dear," she said, "with the guns and ammunition. They want a word with you." She disappeared again.

"I'm sorry," said the Constable, his manner as kind and unruffled as when he began, "I must get on. There's a lot to get ready for Saturday, as you can see. But thank you for coming anyway—it's always best to report anything you think is suspicious—even though as often as not there's no cause for concern."

He showed them firmly out.

"It's a shame about the seals, I know," he said condescendingly, "but they're only dumb animals. Don't worry, there'll still be plenty left—certainly won't do them any harm to cream off surplus numbers. And almost everyone else in the village is agreed about it, you know—so there's no going against the majority, now is there?"

"I almost exploded!" cried Katie as they walked back. "Oooh!" she clenched her fists. "The way he twisted everything round! Why should he just refuse to see sense, Tom?"

"Well," said Tom, "it took something pretty drastic to make *you* change your mind, didn't it? Anyway, that's our last chance gone Kate. We're on our own now. We can't reach the Captain and we can't reach Mrs Northcote-McPherson. We don't even know if either of them will turn up on the day. I've always known what *I'm* going to do, what about you?"

He stopped in the fading twilight and turned to look at her.

"I'll be there too," she said firmly, "surely you realise that by now?"

"But what are you going to do there?" asked Tom again.

A crow flew overhead, croaking loudly and unexpectedly in the dusky stillness.

"Stop the cull," said Katie, "whatever happens and whatever we—I—have to do. I'll make a fool of myself Tom, I'll get into trouble—I don't care. Because the selchies saved my life."

12 The Stranger's Secret

"Are ye ready for the shooting?"

"Ready man? Och, I can't wait to get my hands on the vermin!"

"I'd kill every single one of them if I had my way!"

They were swarming all over the old wooden pier and jostling each other all along the harbour wall; and every minute, more people came hurrying excitedly to join the two hundred villagers who had already gathered there on that sunny Saturday morning. Some of the men were climbing about the boats, stowing guns and clubs and other vicious-looking weapons. The women, wrapped against the wind in headscarves and mackintoshes, stood urging them on excitedly as each fresh load of ammunition appeared.

Noisy groups of children and dogs were playing by the harbour office; but Tom and Katie were not with them. They hovered silently on the edge of the crowd where a row of stiff, toothless old men sat on the bollards, listening and watching steadily from bright, sunken eyes and muttering sadly in Gaelic—the old tongue— under their breath.

At eleven o'clock precisely a car drove up and Mr Edward da Silva got out. A rousing cheer went up as he swaggered his way to the front and it grew even louder when he climbed up onto a makeshift rostrum of several upturned fish-crates.

Smooth-jowled and arrogant he stood there, one hand on his slim, well-tailored hip, the other raised to hush his clamouring supporters.

"My friends!" His voice rang out across the harbour. "I am delighted to see that so many of you have turned out today to claim back your rightful heritage of fish which has been snatched from you by a plague of seals."

Several people started to clap in a slow rhythm: "Kill the seals! Kill the seals! Kill the seals!"

"They're out there on the rocks now," said Mr da Silva, "breeding. The place is crawling with seal-pups. Thousands of them! Another generation of parasites to take your fish!"

"Aye, that's right, parasites!"

"They're the ones we want—get the pups!"

"What I propose to do," Mr da Silva went on, "is to divide you good people into teams, so that each one can attack a different rock."

"Tom," whispered Katie, "we've got to do something. Quickly!"

They looked around the crowd: every eager face was turned to da Silva, every angry mouth was cheering, every man's hand was twitching, restless to pull the trigger that might bring the fish back to their local waters.

106

Only the grey-whiskered old sea-dogs shook their heads in dissent and spat wearily into puddles of brine by their feet.

"I can't see Mrs Northcote-McPherson anywhere, can you?" said Katie, standing on tiptoe.

"Never mind," hissed Tom. "Come on, they'll be setting off in a few minutes and then it'll be too late. You'd better start kicking up a fuss—shout or scream or something—anything that'll hold things up."

"Why me? What shall I say? I . . ."

"You promised you would! Come on, *hurry*!" He half-pushed her to climb onto the low stone wall of the harbour. "Say anything—it doesn't matter what, so long as it's really loud!"

So Katie, in a daze of panic, held her breath and counted silently up to ten; then she opened her mouth and yelled out as piercingly as she could:

"Stop! It's lies! It's a fake!"

At once the hum of chatter stopped, Edward da Silva broke off in mid-sentence and two hundred pairs of eyes turned to look at her.

Katie blushed scarlet from ear to ear; across the sea of people she could see her own father gazing at her in horrified amazement. She tried to say something more, or to move from her conspicuous position; but her tongue felt heavy as lead in her mouth and her legs had turned to jelly.

Then Tom's voice piped up:

"We've got proof—to show that it's all a sham— and you mustn't kill the seals!"

A titter rippled through the throng. Edward da Silva watched them both from narrowed eyes and then suddenly he burst into a raucous laugh.

"Ha ha ha!" he sniggered. "Ladies and gentlemen, I do believe that we have here the 'Defendants of the Seals', young knights in shining armour come to plead the villains' cause. Well: have we time to hear their story?"

"Come on then," called someone above the laughter, "what have you got to show us—a performing seal from a circus?"

Katie stood her ground and stared unwaveringly back at Edward da Silva, while Tom hopped from one foot to another with impotent rage. But their delaying tactics had paid off, for now a taxi came screeching round the corner, its passenger jumped out and slammed the door; and then the clear, mellow tones of Mrs Northcote-McPherson were booming out:

"Mr da Silva! You may recall that when you addressed the village two weeks ago, we exchanged a few words and that I promised we should meet again before all was said and done. I have left you in peace until today, so perhaps now you would be good enough to spare me a few minutes of your time?"

Edward da Silva did not bat an eyelid. His voice was crisp as he replied, "Madam, I'm so sorry, but I don't remember you at all."

Another ripple of laughter ran through the crowd. Katie and Tom could just see the iron-grey curls that topped Mrs Northcote-McPherson's tall, handsome head.

"What a pity," she retorted, and her voice was as cool and calm as his. "Perhaps you have a very bad memory for faces? But I, fortunately, have a particularly good one. Which is why, when I was recently chased at sea by a speed-boat which I am sure was trying to sink me, I immediately recognised the man who was steering it."

Katie gasped.

"It was you Mr da Silva," said Mrs Northcote-McPherson, "it was you who nearly had me—and a young girl—drowned!"

"Come on now, lady," someone called, "let's get on with the cull!"

Edward da Silva shrugged. "Madam, I am afraid you have made a great mistake. Now, back to business. I have ordered one hundred rifles..."

"Just a minute, just a minute." Mrs Northcote-McPherson's commands were uttered with the assurance of a general. "Would you kindly allow me to finish? So—you know nothing of this shocking incident? Well, let me elaborate. I was out investigating a ship, Mr da Silva, about which I had heard strange rumours concerned with the sudden disappearance of our coastal fish; not to mention the emission of bizarre noises and the suspicious veil of secrecy when anyone tried to identify its whereabouts or business."

Katie and Tom waited, hearts beating fast. They could see PC Stuart, beetroot-coloured with sur-

prise standing below Mr da Silva avoiding their eyes
and fingering his truncheon nervously.

"This ship is called the *Vagabond*, and it is
registered in Amsterdam," said Mrs Northcote-
McPherson. "Perhaps that clarifies things for you a
little?"

If you looked carefully at Edward da Silva, you
could just see the colour draining out of his face,
very slowly, until his black moustache stood out
thick and sinister against skin that was ghostly pale.

"Since that memorable chase I have been making
lengthy enquiries," Mrs Northcote-McPherson continued. "In the end I was compelled to travel
abroad. I discovered a lot in a short time; such as
that the *Vagabond* is registered in the name of Silva
Enterprises — sir!

"I also learned a lot about you, Mr da Silva. I
understand that you have made a great deal of
money from selling skins and furs; and that you
spent five years in prison for illegally dealing in the
skins of the almost extinct Spanish lynx. Now — I
wonder what is the current market price for the fur
of the grey seal pup? No doubt by selling the ones
that you kill today you hope to increase your
fortune even more!"

There was a stunned silence: a shaking of heads
and whispered questions. Then, quite unexpectedly,
it was broken by the splish-splash of oars as a small
boat rowed steadily into view and entered the
harbour.

Mr da Silva was momentarily thrown off balance

and his lips moved in speechless anger.

Abruptly, the sound of rowing ceased. There was the slap of rope against wood as the oarsman tied up at the end of the pier. A lone figure, carrying a large, brown leather case, climbed out of the boat and began to limp towards the crowd.

And then everyone began to nudge their neighbours and murmur in disbelief.

"Katie!" cried Tom, "look, can you see? It's the Captain! The Captain's come ashore!"

He came slowly, but with great dignity; even the way that he limped was dignified. He was wearing full uniform and black rubber gum-boots; from under his peaked hat his curious, pale hair flowed like a mane. He looked unwaveringly ahead with the determination of an ambassador who has travelled interminable distances to deliver an important message.

The other keepers had brought back plenty of stories about him from his lonely, white beacon; but now, for the first time, here he was in the flesh—the strange recluse who had not once visited the mainland for eleven years! Was it any wonder that every eye was glued to him, that every woman, man and child just stared and stared?

"My dear fellow!" called Mrs Northcote-McPherson when he was near enough to hear her, "a hundred thousand welcomes! Have you come to our rescue after all?"

The Captain saluted her gravely, saying as he pushed his way through the dumb-struck crowd.

"'Twas the selchies, Ma'am. I would not make a promise to ye, but I have no power to refuse the selchies."

Meanwhile, Edward da Silva had seized upon this diversion to pull himself together. You would have thought that nothing had ever ruffled him as he announced:

"My friends, I was discussing the allocation of rifles for the cull . . ."

"Mr da Silva, sir!" exclaimed Mrs Northcote-McPherson in a voice that would have made even a saint feel guilty. The Captain was now at her side.

"Is this the gentleman?" he asked as if the three of them were quite alone.

Mrs Northcote-McPherson nodded.

The crowd waited.

Tom climbed onto the wall next to Katie in order to get a better view.

"May I speak?" asked the Captain.

"I wish you would!" called a woman's voice. "There's funny things going on here and it's about time we knew what it's all about!"

The Captain opened his case and took from it a tape recorder.

"In the dead of night," he cried, "I have often heard this sound floating to me across the ocean. Listen to it if ye will—and see if it does not make your very hearts tremble!"

He switched on the tape: at once the air was filled with that moaning echo, that weird, whistling summons that Katie and Tom had heard through the mist on the lighthouse island.

The Captain stopped the tape and his thin, clear Celtic voice rang out again in the shocked hush:

"I know ye are all wanting to rid yourselves of the selchies. But they are helpless victims just like ye! I have seen them when this terrible call was upon them, swimming outwards to the emptiest reaches of the ocean like slaves to their master.

"But it was not intended for their ears. For one night when this call was ringing out across the water, I saw by the beam from my tower that the sea was full of fish. And all of the fish were swimming to that very sound!

"This call that you have heard is the most ancient of all sounds. It cannot fail to move any living thing that hears it, least of all those creatures whose home is in the depths of the sea from whence it first was born."

"Look," whispered Katie, "just look at Mr da Silva now!"

He was running a hand through his hair; he was hunting for something in the pocket of his jacket; his eyes were shifting here and there; he was straightening his tie. He could not stay still for one moment, for he was trying to hide his shaking hands and the ashen agitation in his face.

The Captain continued: "At length, when all was quiet again, the selchies did turn back. But as for the fish, I never did see a single one return."

"My dear Captain," cried Mrs Northcote-McPherson, "where were they heading?"

"Ma'am," said the Captain, "I could not rest until I had the answer. So another time when this crazy movement was upon the sea, I rowed out in its wake. I had no light to guide me: only the stars and three selchies swimming by my side and drawn, as before, to the call.

"At last, when dawn was creeping up, the selchies did turn back with fear. Because looming before us on the skyline was a great, dark ship. And from the hull of this ship came the noise."

"Ha!" exclaimed Mrs Northcote-McPherson.

The whole crowd was holding its breath. Nobody even coughed or sneezed: they stood there in the breezy sunshine like statues.

"I took my camera with me," said the Captain. "I have made negatives and positives in the dark-room at the top of my tower, and now I have enlarged them and suffered to bring them ashore so that all the world may see the truth!"

From his leather bag he pulled out, one at a time, three black-and-white, poster-sized photographs and held them above his head, twisting slowly around, so that everyone should have the chance to see.

There was the ominous mass of the windowless ship with *Vagabond—Amsterdam* printed clearly upon its side!

There, protruding from her prow, was a huge, shovel-like iron scoop!

And there, in the last picture, was clearly shown a dense, wriggling shoal of fish, being scooped up—

like rubbish—into the hold of the ship!

The Captain's voice was shrill as he replaced the photographs and ripped the cap from his head so that his wild, white locks flew suddenly in the wind.

"'Tis not the selchies who have been taking your fish! 'Tis this ship that has been calling them from your waters and the evil man who owns it who has been destroying them! Yet ye would all kill the selchies, blinded by your madness—while this man here will grow rich from the sale of their skins and your fish!"

And now uproar broke out, the loud, stirring rage of people who have been trapped by their own folly. But in the midst of all the shouting, Tom was suddenly pinching Katie's arm so hard that she almost screamed.

"Kate, quick! He's trying to get away!"

For while the crowd was mesmerised by the photos, Edward da Silva had slipped quietly down from his rostrum and now he was inching his way to where his car stood open and ready, twenty yards from the bollards.

"Yes, I can see him! That's his car—the sports car. We might just beat him to it."

Leaping over feet, elbowing people aside, they got there less than thirty seconds before Mr da Silva, whilst on the quayside anger was turning to action:

"Where's da Silva?"

"Get the villain!"

"He's gone—where is he?"

Katie was at the door and pressing the metal lock: it sprang open more easily than she had expected. The keys were hanging in readiness in the dashboard. She reached out but, just as her fingers were closing over them, she felt a rough, heavy hand on her shoulder.

"Give them to me, you..." snarled Edward da Silva.

"Tom—catch!"

With sudden strength she twisted out of his hold and flung the keys as hard and as far as she could. Miraculously, they landed in Tom's cupped hands, and at once Mr da Silva released her and turned to Tom, his shrewd eyes taking in this new situation with the quick glance of one who is accustomed to trouble.

The chorus of voices was deafening now.

"Don't let him get away!"

"Who saw him go?"

"There he is—over there—look!"

And there too was Mrs Northcote-McPherson's voice, calm and confident as ever: "Have the police arrived yet?"

The car was his only hope of escape. With an evil, blood-curdling cry he lurched for Tom; Tom side-stepped quickly out of his way, almost over-balanced, caught Katie's voice yelling, "Throw them, throw them!" and, in a flash of comprehension, hurled the keys out of da Silva's reach and into the harbour where they sank into the water with a resounding splash.

"He's here, he's here!" shouted Katie as PC Stuart, gulping audibly, came hurrying out towards them; but da Silva was already vaulting over the bollards and running, fast as a cheetah, up the main street.

Just at that moment they heard a wailing of sirens as two blue police-cars came hurtling round the corner. There was a quick scuffle on the cobbled pavement and then they were driving smoothly away again, with Edward da Silva in hand-cuffs, leaving two hundred startled people blinking at each other on the quayside in the autumn sunshine.

13 A Promise Fulfilled

The first frost had fallen and the countryside was sharp and shimmering in the bright, early morning light when Tom went running down to the harbour, humming loudly to himself.

How different everything was now in the village! Mrs McCodrum stood on the doorstep of her store, all smiles at anyone who went by, while her husband helped PC Stuart drape gaily-coloured flags and bunting down the lamp-posts of the main street. On the quayside the first catch had already been landed and two fat women were haggling cheerfully over a box of herrings with a red-faced lad in an oilskin apron. Every boat was occupied and everyone was hard at work, mending nets, cleaning tools, stowing oil-drums; some were even busy with pots of paint so that the whole harbour looked quite festive with all the wet, gleaming colours. Angus Dougall, ruling up the pages of a brand new record book, was puffing out huge clouds of tobacco smoke and constantly shouting greetings through the open door of his hut. And the air was full of singing: shanties and ballads, drinking songs, hums and whistles: the whole village seemed to have a tune on its lips today!

A formation of wild ducks passed overhead, their long necks stretched out as they headed south. They too were singing on their way.

At last Tom saw Katie coming to meet him as she had promised she would; and she alone in all the world did not look happy at all, but dawdled on her way, one hand in her coat pocket, the other bouncing a ball in front of her joylessly as she came.

"Hello Tom," she said.

Tom took a deep breath, swallowed hard and did his best to match her mood.

"Hello Kate."

They wandered over to one of the boats and stood watching its crew loading on the orange plastic crates in which they would bring back the fish.

"Isn't it great?" he said. "Everything's just like it always was. Plenty of fish now!"

"You'll miss it Tom," said Katie, "won't you?"

"Perhaps," said Tom guardedly.

She turned on him: "Oh you will, I know you will! You'll miss it all in the city."

Tom said nothing.

"Is it tomorrow you're leaving?"

He shrugged. "Perhaps."

"I don't believe you even care," said Katie. "I care more about it than you do. I'll have to go out boating and hiking all on my own, and you'll actually be *liking* the city!"

"Not true," said Tom; and he unwrapped a piece

of chewing gum and bit hard on it because he did not want to betray what he was thinking through any movement of his face.

"Hey look," he said suddenly, "isn't that Mrs Northcote-McPherson over there?"

Sure enough, the noble lady herself was standing on the wall by the entrance to the harbour, clad in a long, full, heather-coloured tweed cape. She saw them looking at her and waved heartily; but she seemed to be watching out to sea for something and did not beckon them to approach.

Very soon, a small boat with a curiously familiar shape rowed into the harbour and moored up at an iron ring by her feet; and then a slim, white-haired figure climbed nimbly up the old, seaweed-covered steps and shook Mrs Northcote-McPherson vigorously by the hand.

"Gracious!" exclaimed Katie, "it's the Captain again! Come to see *her*!"

They made an odd pair as they walked along the harbour wall together, for she was at least a head taller than the Captain; yet his stride, long and loping like a hare's despite his limp, could more than keep up with hers. They were soon deep in conversation like old friends; every so often they stopped and the Captain pointed out to sea or waved his arms about to make a point. Once he unfolded a large roll of blue paper he was carrying which seemed to be a sort of chart of the ocean and they both pored carefully over it for a moment before continuing on their way.

"Good morning Thomas and Katherine," beamed Mrs Northcote-McPherson regally as they came sweeping past.

"Ah, 'tis good to see ye again my wee friends, on a bright and happy morning like this," said the Captain, and he winked at them—a big, smiling wink, the like of which they had never received from him before.

But they did not stop to talk.

"We'll be in touch," called Mrs Northcote-McPherson over her shoulder. "You're both to come to tea with me next week. I've an enormous hamper just arrived from Harrods in London, and I'm planning a small celebration party to help me eat it up!"

"Well," cried Katie as they disappeared down the road, "talk about selchie-magic! Fancy the old Captain coming ashore again—and to see *her* too!"

Tom looked at her.

"Do you believe in selchie-magic Kate?" he asked.

"Not really . . . No, of course I don't! I'm sure everything's got a simple, normal explanation when it comes down to it, aren't you?" she said. "Like that weird noise—I *did* think it was something spooky at first, but then it just turned out to be a factory ship. As for the selchies—well, they're . . . they're only *seals*, Tom. I'm ever so glad they're all still alive and rearing their pups in peace—but it's only old folk and people like the

Captain—and you—who believe they're anything more than plain, ordinary animals."

"Perhaps..." said Tom; and there was something maddening about the way he kept saying 'perhaps'.

"You've got something to say, haven't you?" said Katie, "so come on, let's hear it."

"Well," said Tom, spitting out his chewing gum with relief, "you know what I told you about the day when we had a row and I found a selchie waiting on the beach with a dead one beside it?"

She nodded.

"I didn't tell you everything. Not the last bit. Because...oh, because I knew *you'd* just think it was nonsense. But now I can. Because it's not."

"Well?"

"You see, just as I was going, the selchie gave me a strange look. Long and searching . . . somehow sort of meaningful. I know it was trying to tell me something . . . something . . ."

Katie was already giggling and had opened her mouth to speak, but he cried,

"No, shut up and listen! It's not stupid, wait till you've heard it all! It was as if it were making a promise—in return for my help, because I'd sworn to stop the cull. And now of course they're all safe again and Mrs McCodrum says the selchies never forget . . ."

But Katie was laughing and shaking her head.

"All right then, let me explain."

He paused to clear his throat and then went on:

"You know what my dad's like—stubborn as a

lump of old granite when he's made up his mind. He got a letter this morning from the factory in Glasgow where he's got this job, with a contract in it. Telling him to start the week after next. I couldn't face breakfast when I saw what it was, but I was just going out when he called me back. You'll never guess what he did, Kate: he tore the letter up, contract and all, into tiny bits!"

Katie's mouth dropped open and she grabbed him by the shoulders. "Does this mean...?"

"Oh yes, we're not going now! Now the fish are back, there's no need to leave the village at all! 'They can keep their blasted job,' said my dad, 'I've changed my mind and we're staying here!' I've never known him like it before! 'I was wrong about those seals,' he said, 'so I might as well double it and admit I was wrong in moving out.' My mum was so amazed she let the porridge burn a great big hole in the saucepan. She said it was the first mistake he'd ever owned up to in all the years they'd been married!"

For a small, bright moment Katie was struck dumb. She looked at Tom, then down at the bustling harbour and finally out to sea, past the distant lighthouse, shimmering in the frosty haze, to the lonely skerries where hundreds of small, hooting seal pups would be taking their first diving lessons in the grey ocean.

"Well!" she stammered. "They're supposed to have saved the Captain, aren't they? And I *know* they saved me and Mrs Northcote-McPherson. And

123

now they've made your dad change his mind and saved you from moving..."

He looked at her expectantly.

"So of course, I'll have to believe in selchie-magic now, won't I?"

Some other Puffins

CASEY DRAWS THE LINE
AND OTHER STORIES
Kit Hood and Linda Schuyler with Eve Jennings

There's never a dull moment in Degrassi Street, and here are three more adventures featuring the irrepressible Kids.

BOSS OF THE POOL   *Robin Klein*

Shelley has to spend her evenings at the hostel where her mother works, and, to her horror, mentally handicapped Ben attaches himself to her from the start. But although he's terrified of the pool, he comes to watch her swimming. And despite herself, Shelley begins to help him overcome his fear.

ROB'S PLACE   *John Rowe Townsend*

It's through Mike that Rob learns to escape from his everyday life which he is finding more and more difficult to cope with. He discovers Paradise – a fantastic place which is all his own and where he is master. But can he manage to control his fantasy or will his Paradise become a nightmare?

THE WELL   *Gene Kemp*

A secret hideaway, dragons in the well, broken vases and hidden Easter eggs: these are just some of the vivid memories which Annie Sutton (alias Gene Kemp) recalls in these hilarious and perceptive tales of childhood.

COME BACK SOON *Judy Gardiner*

Val's family seem quite an odd bunch and their life is hectic but happy. But then Val's mother walks out on them and Val's carefree life is suddenly quite different. This is a moving but funny story.

AMY'S EYES *Richard Kennedy*

When a doll changes into a man it means that anything might happen ... and in this magical story all kinds of strange and wonderful things do happen to Amy and her sailor doll, the Captain. Together they set off on a fantastic journey on a quest for treasure more valuable than mere gold.

ASTERCOTE *Penelope Lively*

Astercote village was destroyed by plague in the fourteenth century and Mair and her brother, Peter, find themselves caught up in a strange adventure when an ancient superstition is resurrected.

THE HOUNDS OF THE MÓRRÍGAN
Pat O'Shea

When the Great Queen Mórrígan, evil creature from the world of Irish mythology, returns to destroy the world, Pidge and Brigit are the children chosen to thwart her. How they go about it makes an hilarious, moving story, full of original and unforgettable characters.

COME SING, JIMMY JO *Katherine Paterson*

An absorbing story about eleven-year-old Jimmy Jo's rise to stardom, and the problem of coping with fame.

JELLYBEAN   *Tessa Duder*

A sensitive modern novel about Geraldine, alias 'Jellybean', who leads a rather solitary life as the only child of a single parent. She's tired of having to fit in with her mother's busy schedule, but a new friend and a performance of *The Nutcracker Suite* change everything.

THE PRIESTS OF FERRIS   *Maurice Gee*

Susan Ferris and her cousin, Nick, return to the world of O which they had saved from the evil Halfmen, only to find that O is now ruled by cruel and ruthless priests. Can they save the inhabitants of O from tyranny? An action-packed and gripping story by the author of prize-winning *The Halfmen of O*.

THE SEA IS SINGING   *Rosalind Kerven*

In her seaside Shetland home, Tess is torn between the plight of the whales and loyalty to her father and his job on the oil rig. A haunting and thought-provoking novel.

BACK HOME   *Michelle Magorian*

A marvellously gripping story of an irrepressible girl's struggle to adjust to a new life. Twelve-year-old Rusty, who had been evacuated to the United States when she was seven, returns to the grey austerity of post-war Britain.

THE BEAST MASTER   *Andre Norton*

Spine-chilling science fiction – treachery and revenge! Hosteen Storm is a man with a mission to find and punish Brad Quade, the man who killed his father long ago on Terra, the planet where life no longer exists.